"Jake, the woman you met that night wasn't the real me," Nila said. "I'm not like that at all."

"Not like what?" he asked, his lips teasing her earlobe.

Her mind whirled with momentary dizziness. She snaked her arms up to his shoulders and held on tight. "Passionate. Reckless. Free."

He smiled. "Yes, you are. You've just been hiding it behind baggy clothes and glasses. All you needed was the right man to set that part of you free—"

"What do you want from me?" She shut her eyes, trying to stop the flood of desire that raged through her body.

"Everything . . ."

WHAT ARE *LOVESWEPT* ROMANCES?

They are stories of true romance and touching emotion. We believe those two very important ingredients are constants in our highly sensual and very believable stories in the *LOVESWEPT* line. Our goal is to give you, the reader, stories of consistently high quality that may sometimes make you laugh, sometimes make you cry, but are always fresh and creative and contain many delightful surprises within their pages.

Most romance fans read an enormous number of books. Those they truly love, they keep. Others may be traded with friends and soon forgotten. We hope that each *LOVESWEPT* romance will be a treasure—a "keeper." We will always try to publish

LOVE STORIES YOU'LL NEVER FORGET
BY AUTHORS YOU'LL ALWAYS REMEMBER

The Editors

Loveswept 579

Theresa Gladden
Bad Company

BANTAM BOOKS
NEW YORK · TORONTO · LONDON · SYDNEY · AUCKLAND

BAD COMPANY

A Bantam Book / November 1992

If you would be interested in receiving protective vinyl
covers for your Loveswept books, please write to this address
for information:

Loveswept
Bantam Books
P.O. Box 985
Hicksville, NY 11802

ISBN 0-553-44178-7

Published simultaneously in the United States and Canada

Bantam Books are published by Bantam Books, a division of
Bantam Doubleday Dell Publishing Group, Inc. Its trademark,
consisting of the words "Bantam Books" and the portrayal of
a rooster, is Registered in U.S. Patent and Trademark Office
and in other countries. Marca Registrada. Bantam Books, 666
Fifth Avenue, New York, New York 10103.

With love and gratitude to Bob and Eileen Gladden, Sandra Barganier, Lota Weichsel, Rose and Glen Rosamond.

With gratitude to Debbie and Richard Moore for allowing me to re-create the friendly, warm environment of The Bookstore, for hours of pleasant conversation, and for countless cups of terrific coffee.

With gratitude to Rena Vaughn for the tour of Danville and Millionaire's Row.

One

At first glance, Jake Madison thought she looked like a good-time girl wrapped in black velvet and tied with an emerald-green satin bow.

Her dress was quite a come-on, a showcase for shapely legs, creamy shoulders, and a body that promised endless delights. No man alive could resist the temptation to untie that big bow and slowly unwrap the package.

As Jake continued to stare at her, an alarm sounded in the back of his mind. It was kind of a sixth sense, finely honed from years spent living on the extreme edge. It usually warned him when a job was about to go sour. It had never been triggered before by the sight of a desirable woman, and he felt a surge of adrenaline kick in. To get a closer look at the woman, he walked over to the railing that separated the bar from the gambling floor of the Bahamas Queen Casino.

Desirable was an inadequate description, he decided, resting his fingers on the polished brass rail. She wasn't the voluptuous type, yet there was a subtle invitation in the small curves of her high breasts, gently flaring hips, and pale skin bared by her off-the-shoulder dress.

Gold was buried in her spice-brown hair. The rich mass curved on each side of her heart-shaped face, the ends caressing her shoulders.

As though sensing she was being watched, she looked toward the bar and directly at him. For an endless moment Jake absorbed the full force of her gaze. Sexual energy burned the distance between them. It was followed by a flash of primitive recognition that almost rocked him off his feet and overrode the alarm still ringing in his head. He tightened his grip on the railing as shock waves traveled up his spine and exploded in his head.

"Your drink, sir."

Jake stiffened and turned to find a cocktail waitress standing beside him.

Shaken by the depth of her reaction to the man standing at the bar, Nila quickly melted into the crowd.

The moment she had met his night-dark gaze, something strange had happened to her, something so compelling and blatantly sensual, it made her head swim and her heart flutter. She had never felt so exhilarated and frightened at the same time. And for one crazy, timeless instant she could have sworn he was experiencing the same startling sensation.

That was ridiculous, she told herself. Men simply didn't react that way to plain old Nila Shepherd. And yet . . .

She smiled with surprise and pleasure. Maybe the fantasy she'd set out to create was working! She certainly didn't look like plain old Nila Shepherd from Danville, Virginia.

Tonight she was a temptress in a drop-dead dress, spiky three-inch heels, and dangling emerald earrings. No one could possible know the dress was borrowed, or that the shoes pinched her toes, or that the emeralds were as phony as the sophistication and self-assurance she projected.

For the first time since setting foot on the island, she was glad she had allowed her best friend Angie to bully her into coming to Freeport to get away from the pitying eyes of well-meaning friends.

Once again, Angie's parting advice rang in her ears. "Let your hair down and take a walk on the wild side." Nila didn't intend to take that walk, but she could pretend for a little while. A few hours of living a fantasy was harmless enough.

Remembering the way the man at the bar had looked at her, she felt her smile broaden into a grin. What a great start to her fantasy! If she knew who he was, she'd send him a thank-you note for giving her feminine ego a much-needed shot in the arm.

Feeling lucky, she headed for the slot machines.

By the time Jake paid the tab and claimed his drink, his inner warning system was silent. With a single glance he saw that the woman in the black and emerald dress had disappeared into the crowd.

He fought the temptation to search for her, telling himself every resort on the Grand Bahama Island had its share of good-time girls. Maybe she was one of them. Maybe she wasn't. No one knew better than he that things and people weren't always what they seemed.

It would be best to forget her. He raised his drink to his lips. The smooth blended Scotch whisky coursed down his throat. Lowering the glass, he stared discontentedly at its contents. He didn't particularly care for Scotch, but it went well with the role he'd chosen for the evening.

Unbidden, a picture of the unknown woman formed in his mind. She would go perfectly with his suit, the drink, the persona. But forget it, he told himself again. He didn't intend to take the game that far.

The game. He'd spent the last two hours giving a satisfactory performance as a well-heeled VIP player as he mentally recorded all he saw and heard. An hour from now, a year from now, Jake knew he would be able to recall accurately the casino's layout, from the positions of the tables to the carpet's Moorish motif, as well as describe the clientele he'd chosen at random to observe.

The information as well as the playacting was pointless, and it had long lost its entertainment value. He wasn't on the job anymore. That part of his life was over.

The restless feeling of being suspended in limbo returned to him with a vengeance. It had haunted him since he'd resigned from the job. And it was growing stronger.

He swallowed the rest of the Scotch. As he turned to set the glass down on an empty table, he caught a glimpse of his scowling face in the mirror behind the bar.

What the hell was he doing there, pretending to be something he wasn't?

What the hell was he going to do without the job?

Why did he feel so damn lost and alone?

Abruptly, Jake walked through the bar and down the steps to the gaming area. Not understanding why but feeling compelled to do so, he went in search of the woman in black velvet and green satin.

It didn't take him long to find her. She was pumping quarters into a one-armed bandit. Instead of approaching her immediately, he positioned himself where he could watch her without being noticed.

Nila put another quarter in the slot. The machine clanged and whirred to life when she pulled the lever. Colorful images of lemons, oranges, cherries, and bells spun madly.

The two lemons and the bell that finally clicked into place reminded her of her mother's three ex-husbands. Thinking about the third spouse, she shook her head. The poor man had been a major ding-a-ling, who had stood on a railroad track one night and dared a train to hit him. Which it had. Her older sister, Mary, was following in their mother's disastrous marital footsteps.

A flashing sign invited Nila to try her luck again. She sighed. Her luck with gambling wasn't any better than her luck with men. According to everyone in her hometown, if it weren't for bad luck, the Shepherd women wouldn't have any luck at all with men. The men in their lives had a way of breaking their hearts, of disappearing, deserting, or dying.

She reluctantly picked up her clutch bag. Her wicked night of gambling was over. It had taken her less than half an hour to lose the money she'd allotted herself.

"Play it one more time."

She whirled around to find the man she'd seen at the bar standing behind her. From a distance, she'd thought him attractive. Seeing him up close, she realized her assessment was way off the mark.

He had an aggressive face with strong features

and a brooding sensuality that would make a him a dramatic choice for any photographer or sculptor. Somewhere in his genetic pool was a bit of Native American, she decided, taking note of prominent cheekbones, a long broad nose, and a bronze skin tone. Judging from the lines of experience marking the corners of his deep-set ebony eyes, she placed his age in the upper range of the thirty-something scale.

His hair added to his aura of sensuality. It was blacker than Satan's heart. He wore it combed back from his wide forehead and tied in a ponytail with a leather thong. The ends just brushed the collar of his expertly tailored suit.

He was the kind of man her mother and sister would absolutely adore—bad to the bone, from the blood-red ruby stud in his pierced ear to the polished sheen of his shoes. He was also the kind of man Nila had spent her life avoiding.

"What did you say?" she asked, hoping he didn't notice the way she gulped in a breath of air.

"Play it one more time," he repeated quietly. His voice, rich and intimately low, gave her chills. It had almost as much of a dangerous effect on her as his eyes. Those gleaming dark eyes were watchful, calculating, seeming to absorb and analyze without giving away any hint of what he was thinking.

"Oh no, I can't," she said. "The machine ate my last quarter. I lost ten dollars. I haven't been very lucky tonight."

"I have a feeling that your luck is about to change. My name is Jake Madison." He smiled. The hint of a dimple in his right cheek softened the sharklike quality of that smile and made Nila feel a little weak in the knees. She'd always been a sucker for dimples.

"Nila Shepherd," she responded as her gaze traveled from his face to the coin resting in the palm of his smooth, well-shaped hand. "I think you're wasting your money, but if you insist." She shrugged and reached for the quarter.

When her fingertips grazed his palm, he surprised her by curving his fingers over hers. His hand was large and warm. Although he exerted no pressure, she could feel the strength of his long, tapered fingers. For one dizzy moment, she shocked herself by imagining what they would feel like sliding over her bare skin.

She withdrew her hand from his grasp as she forced her wanton thoughts away. Turning, she slipped the coin into the slot and pulled the lever. The images on the wheels spun round and round in a frantic rush. Three plump ruby-red cherries clicked into place and quarters rained down into the pan beneath the machine.

She looked at Jake in astonishment. "We won twenty-five dollars! How did you know that would happen?"

"I didn't. It was just a lucky guess."

She smiled up at him as he helped her fill a plastic container with coins. "Do you really believe in luck?"

"I believe in luck and in divine providence. I believe in listening to my instincts. And, Nila, I believe my first impression of you was completely off base."

She stared blankly at him. "What impression?"

"I thought you were a beautiful party doll."

Beautiful? Her eyes widened in wonder. At best, she knew people considered her the passably attractive one in a family of beautiful women. Then a pink flush spread over her cheeks. "Party doll!" she repeated as she digested the term and its unsavory connotation. "Why would you think I was a . . ." She couldn't finish the thought.

"The come-and-get-me statement your dress makes fooled me for a second," he said apologetically.

"Angie told me it was elegant and sophisticated."

His gaze slid from her bared shoulders, to the ivory column of her throat, then to the intriguing swell of her breasts above the dress's low neckline. "I don't know who Angie is, but her idea of elegant and sophisticated is a bit on the erotic side. I didn't think you were a party doll for more than a second," he reassured her, smiling. "There was something about that impression that didn't ring true. I found myself very curious and very intrigued. After watching you for a while, I knew you weren't what you appeared to be."

"How did you know?"

He hesitated a moment, studying her confused expression. "I'm not sure I can explain it. There's a softness about you that doesn't fit the image. You don't act like you're on the prowl. When I spoke to you, you weren't flirty or coy." Before she could comprehend what to make of that, he added, "If you've finished gambling for the evening, would you like to take in the casino's floor show with me?"

Nila swallowed uneasily. She wanted very much to say yes, but her ingrained sense of caution asserted itself. "I don't know you."

"Come spend some time with me and discover who I am."

"You could be married and have a houseful of kids for all I know."

His mouth quirked into a brief smile. "I'm not married. I'm alone. You're alone. At least, I assume you are. If you were my lady, I wouldn't let you out of my sight in that dress."

"If that was a compliment, I thank you."

"It was and you're welcome. Will you come with me?"

Still wary, Nila hesitated over her response. She should be trying to resist the lure of the spell this man was casting over her, but her defenses were faltering.

Once again, she thought of Angie's advice. *Take a walk on the wild side.*

Could she do it? she wondered wistfully. Could she let her hair down a little more and accept the invitation in Jake's dangerous eyes?

What if he really was dangerous? What if he really was the kind of bad company she'd avoided all her life?

Jake watch the myriad emotions reflected in Nila's expressive brown eyes. It was obvious her inhibitions were struggling with her desire to go with him, and he was afraid her inhibitions were winning.

Few things in life held any regret for Jake. But his gut instinct told him he would regret it if he allowed Nila to walk away from him. He wanted a chance to know her. He wanted to discover why he felt so drawn to her.

"Come with me, Nila," he said. "You have my promise you'll be safe with me."

"Oh, I'm sure I would be," she responded politely, though she wasn't a hundred percent certain that was true. Yet she wanted it to be true. She wanted to be reckless. She wanted to be with him for a little while longer.

"All right," she said quickly before she could change her mind.

He answered her with a smile, then captured her hand and tucked it into the crook of his arm.

As they walked toward the casino's theater, Nila became aware of the startling sensation of being physically dominated by him. In reality, he wasn't that much taller than her own five feet seven inches, plus another few inches in her spiky high-heeled shoes. She estimated he was about five eleven, give or take a fraction. So it wasn't his height that gave her that feeling.

Maybe it was just the way he moved, she thought. Confidence and sensuality seemed to pour out of him, making her think of dirty dancing and long, slow kisses that lasted until sunrise.

"I think you'll like the floor show," he said, breaking the silence between them. "It's a Las Vegas-type revue. Lots of feathers and flashy costumes. I hear the magician is quite good."

Jake kept up a steady flow of light conversation, and by the time they were seated at a center stage table, he had gathered a little more information about her. She lived in a small town in Virginia. She had arrived on the island two days earlier and, like himself, she was a guest of the Bahamas Queen Resort.

"What would you like to drink?" he asked when a cocktail waitress stopped by the table.

"A Bahama Mama, please."

He ordered two of the island drinks, then leaned back to study his companion. Dark eyes, fringed by black lashes and alight with intelligence and curiosity, dominated her face. Like the rich highlights in her hair, a hint of gold kept her eyes from being merely brown. And she had the softest, most kissable-looking mouth he'd ever seen.

"Jake, may I ask you something rather rude and personal?" Her slender hands twisted together on the table top. "I mean, I don't want to jump to any wrong conclusions about you."

He listened to her say his name and tried to remember the last time anyone had asked his permission before posing a nosy question. Unexpectedly, he found it as refreshing as her lilting, sweet-as-a-Georgia-peach accent. "I'm not easily offended. Be as rude and personal as you want."

He sat forward. "I'm equally curious about you. Will you let me ask rude, personal questions too?"

"You may ask. But I doubt you'll find the answers very interesting. Until recently, I've managed to tiptoe through life quietly and uneventfully."

"I find that hard to believe."

She laughed, and Jake liked the sound of it. He could easily get used to it and the glow it brought to her eyes.

"I swear it's true," she said. "My mother and sister go through life creating tidal waves. I just float along in the wake and try not to drown."

"Do they live in the same town as you do?"

"No, thank heaven," she said, the laughter fading from her eyes. "I love them dearly, but they wear me out with their craziness." She paused and looked down. "Jake, are you a professional gambler?"

She looked so serious, he couldn't resist teasing her. "Do I look like one?"

"Professional gambler. Modern-day pirate." She shrugged. "You look like a man who answers questions with questions."

His dimple made a brief appearance. "No, Nila, I don't make my living by gambling. It's just an illusion I chose to create."

"If you're putting on an act, it's a darn good one," she said, eyeing him skeptically.

He laughed. "Thank you."

"Is that all you have to say? How do I know you're really telling me the truth?"

He reached out and captured her wrist. Circled in his big hand, it seemed small and fragile to him. "Because it's true. I know you want to believe me. Just like you want to be with me. But you're afraid to trust me."

"What makes you so sure about that?" Nila asked, trying to appear casual and unconcerned, though her pulse raced from the thrill of his fingers sliding over her wrist.

"Your face gives everything away. Especially your eyes. They reflect your thoughts and emotions like twin mirrors." He let go of her as their drinks arrived. When they were alone again, he said softly, "Nila, I promised you'd be safe with me, and I meant it."

Trapped in his night-dark gaze, she experienced the same exhilarating feeling she'd had the first time their eyes had met. Only this time she wasn't frightened by it. No matter who or what Jake Madison might be, she knew he would never harm her.

She smiled and picked up her glass. "So, you're just indulging in a private fantasy tonight, Mr. Professional Gambler?"

A flash of laughter appeared in his eyes, lasting a second before it dissolved back into his unreadable, watchful expression. "I guess you could say that. What fantasy are you playing out tonight, beautiful lady?"

Disconcerted by his question, she lowered her gaze. "What makes you think I'm acting out a fantasy?"

"As they say, it takes one to know one."

She looked at him again. "I really do tiptoe

through life. At home I'm just plain old Nila Ann Shepherd. Sort of quiet and shy. I can be summed up by the three P's: proper, polite, and prudent." A flush of embarrassment heated her cheeks as she continued, "For once, I just wanted to be impulsive, a little wild and reckless, the kind of beautiful, glamorous woman everyone turns to look at when she walks into a room."

He nodded as if he understood her completely, and it gave her the feeling they were kindred spirits in their efforts to fool the rest of the world. "You don't think I'm being ridiculous?" she asked.

"No, I don't." He saluted her with his glass. "Here's to the most beautiful woman in the room."

She blinked, taken aback. "Thank you, but you don't have to say that. I know I'm not beautiful."

"I think you're beautiful. You certainly turned my head when you walked into the casino. I couldn't take my eyes off you. I came looking for you and I found you."

The quiet satisfaction in his voice made her feel as if he had not only come looking for her, but that he had claimed her in some strange way. "Yes," she whispered as a small tremor went through her. "Yes, you did. Who are you, Jake?"

Two

Jake regretted the wariness he read in Nila's eyes. Regretted it because he now understood what his inner alarm had been trying to tell him. He was strongly, incomprehensibly, attracted to her, this woman who didn't see herself as beautiful. For a moment he was at a loss as to how to gain her trust. He didn't want to use his manipulative skills to overcome her wariness. He wanted to be straight with her.

He set his glass on the table and locked his gaze on her. "I used to think that my job defined who I am. Now that I'm retired, I've lost that definition. I *was* a federal narcotics agent with the DEA for fifteen years."

"You worked for the Drug Enforcement Administration?"

He nodded. He could see she was relieved he wasn't a criminal. Had he hung out with bad company for so long that he carried the stink of it with him?

"I worked undercover," he continued. "In crack houses, on street corners, in penthouses, in mansions. I've posed as a dope dealer, a priest, a petty hustler, a wealthy middleman, to name but a few. I was good at my job. The tougher the case, the better I liked it. It was my life and my family." He paused, giving her a moment to swallow her shock.

"That's who I was, Nila. Who am I without the job?" He shrugged. "I'm a man who doesn't cheat on his tax returns. I have an apartment in Miami I hardly ever use. The only thing I own of any value to me is a temperamental '66 Ford Mustang convertible."

He sat back to observe the effect of his confession. His heart was hammering against his chest as though he'd just run five miles.

Nila surprised herself by remaining calm and steady beneath his piercing gaze. She had a feeling he expected her to make some kind of harsh judgment of him based on his former career. What she really wanted to say was, "Thank God it's over." The thought of him living in such a treacherous world terrified her. What she actually said was, "Well, that explains your cop's eyes."

"I have cop's eyes? Does that bother you?"

"Oh no, it doesn't bother me at all." From the way he smiled at her, showing his dimple to advantage, she knew he didn't believe her. "Oh, all right," she said with a little laugh. "It bothers me. I have the impression you're always watching and analyzing everything that goes on around you. That's almost as disconcerting as your ability to guard what you're thinking or feeling."

"I'm sorry. It's an occupational hazard."

"When did you retire?"

"Recently."

She detected a note of tension in that single word. She wanted to question him further, but the house lights dimmed, signaling the beginning of the show.

Jake maneuvered his chair around to face the stage. In doing so, his thigh brushed hers. Instead of the usual impersonal feelings that came with accidental body contact, he felt a hot shaft of desire go through him.

He met her startled gaze for a timeless moment. The flow of electricity between them mesmerized him. She was the first to look away, turning her head toward the stage, and the moment was gone.

Whatever was happening between them, Jake didn't believe it was a simple case of physical attraction. It was too powerful, too overwhelming, too damn confusing.

Eight leggy showgirls rushed out on stage in a flurry of feathers and sequins and began cavorting to a lively Broadway tune. Jake ignored them. He was too busy trying to make sense out of something totally senseless.

He studied Nila's profile, liking the delicate curve of her jaw and the way her hair caressed the side of her face. A warm languor stole over him, even as excitement stirred deep within him.

Nila knew he was watching her instead of the show. Warily, she met his gaze. For once, he wasn't bothering to hide what he was feeling. The way he looked at her stole her breath and produced a funny flip-flop sensation in her stomach. He looked at her as though he wanted to take her home and find out what, if anything, she was wearing beneath her vixen's dress. No man had ever looked at her that way! A strange mixture of panic and pleasure rioted along her nerve endings.

Say something, she told herself. Make it witty, or utterly charming and Angie-like. She couldn't think of a single clever comment, though. So she whispered in a breathless voice she hardly recognized as her own, "What's it like being undercover?"

In his mind, Jake had been exploring that question—what it would be like having Nila undercover, the bed covers. Her skin would be soft and supple. Their bodies would fit together perfectly. Her lips would be moist and delectable. His gaze tracked down to the slopes of her breasts.

"Jake?"

He glanced up. She hadn't been echoing his thoughts. Not with that chaste-as-a-church-picnic look on her pretty face. She wanted to know about the job. "What do you think it's like?"

She shook her head. "There you go again. Answering a question with a question."

"Sorry." He smiled. It occurred to him that being with Nila gave him the same feelings the job did. "Running a scam can be exciting." *But not as exciting she was.* "It makes me operate on all cylinders." *And so did she.*

"And the down side?" she asked.

That was something, he thought grimly, something cold and ruthless. Walking with scum hardened the heart and deadened the spirit, making it easy to forget there was anything decent and good to believe in.

"It consumes everything," he said. "You can't share it. You can't afford to get emotionally involved. So you distance yourself, and that distance spills over into the other areas of your life. Going undercover means you abandon your own identity. You're a performer, and you'd better be a good one if you want to live."

"It sounds lonely and terrifying," she whispered.

"Sometimes it is. Most of the time you're too busy living the job to think about it."

"It was difficult for you to quit, wasn't it?"

Her insight surprised him. "Yeah, it was."

She smiled compassionately. "I'm sorry, Jake."

"I'll get over it." He picked up her hand and gave it a squeeze. "I like you, Nila Shepherd." He saw her eyes light up with pleasure over his simple statement and was amazed at how good that made him feel.

For the next hour they were entertained by singers, dancers, jugglers, comedians, and a magician. Through it all, Jake found watching Nila much more interesting. Her eyes sparkled when she laughed, and they widened with faint shock over bawdy jokes or moments of toplessness. Her delight in every act was genuine.

By the time they left the theater and strolled back into the casino, he was willing to bet his life that the only thing phony about Nila was the imitation emeralds swaying from her ears.

He also realized he didn't want the evening to end. His reluctance to say good night to her strengthened with each step. He wasn't in the habit of picking up strange women. It was a stupid thing to do. But Nila made him want to break all the rules. He simply didn't want to let her go.

He came to an abrupt stop.

She glanced at him questioningly.

Without a word he captured her hand and headed not for the nearest exit but to the brass railing by the bar.

"Jake, what—"

He stilled her question by touching her lips with his fingertips. "I don't want to say good night to you. Stay with me another hour."

"I only agreed to see the floor show with you," Nila said, fighting the desire pulsing through her.

"One more hour." His voice deepened to a husky, sexy drawl. "You want to. I can see it in your eyes. The hotel bar is still open. We can go there for a bite to eat, or just dance and talk for a while."

"I'm not sure that would be very wise," she said, though the desire was growing stronger.

"I don't care if it's unwise."

Nila was silent, spellbound by his intense gaze. She had the oddest feeling of being seduced by the rich intimacy of his voice and the ravishing awareness of his thumb stroking her sensitive inner wrist.

Alone in a crowded room. She had never understood that cliché until now. Her awareness of anything was totally consumed by Jake and the invisible cocoon he wove around her.

He raised her hand, and she trembled at the feel of his lips whispering over her skin. "Jake, please!"

"Please what?" he murmured, lifting his other hand to caress her cheek.

She shut her eyes in an effort to deny the exquisite torment. When denial didn't work, she didn't know whether to scream for help or dissolve into a mass of black velvet and emerald satin at his feet.

"The moment I saw you," he murmured, "I knew there was something between us. Don't you feel it too? I'm curious to find out what it is. Aren't you?"

"I wish you wouldn't say things like that." His heated gaze swam into her vision as her eyes fluttered open. She sighed and brushed his hand away from her face. "And don't look at me like that either."

"Like what?" The hint of a smile hovered on his lips.

"Dammit it, Jake. Stop trying to seduce me."

"A little while ago, you said it was disconcerting not to know what I'm thinking and feeling. I'm just trying to show you."

"Forget I said that." She laughed and ruefully shook her head. "I don't think I can take this."

"Yes, you can." His smile became more beguiling. "Nila, sweet Nila, paradise is the loneliest place on earth when you're alone. Would you spend tonight, tomorrow, the rest of your time in paradise with me?"

"You don't want much, do you?" she asked, feeling helplessly, hopelessly caught up in the desire she saw in his hypnotic eyes.

"I'm beginning to think I want it all."

Oh, Jake Madison, she thought, you are truly a dangerous man. And heaven help her, but she wanted to take a once-in-a-lifetime, reckless walk on the wild side with him.

Jake watched one corner of her mouth curve upward. She was giving him a Mona Lisa smile. It made him feel as though she knew some secret, and if he stared at her lips long enough, she might tell it to him and only him.

"Say yes," he urged. "I promise you'll be as safe with me as you want to be. Wherever you lead, I'll follow. Say yes."

Something exquisite and primitive uncurled inside Nila. The need to surrender to it took her physically, emotionally, by storm, and she gave herself up to the inevitable. With a long, tremulous sigh, she said, "Yes."

Minutes later they were strolling through the black garment of night toward the bright lights of their hotel complex across the street. Clouds floated from the face of the moon and moonlight penetrated through the palm trees, falling upon them in radiant silver beams.

Although the November days remained pleasantly warm, the constant tradewinds made the evenings and mornings a bit cool. Nila shivered as the balmy air hit her exposed skin. She was both surprised and pleased by Jake's unexpected gallantry when he removed his suit jacket and draped it around her shoulders.

In companionable silence they walked through the hotel complex to the outdoor minimountain at its center. An extravagant swimming pool with cascading waterfalls surrounded the minimountain. A live calypso band played in the open-air restaurant and bar beside the pool.

Nila felt the pulsating beat of Bahamian drums enter her bloodstream as Jake guided her toward a table near one of the waterfalls.

A waiter hurried over as soon as they were seated. "Are you hungry?" Jake asked her.

She shook her head.

The waiter offered Jake the island specialty, conch fritters, pronouncing the word "conch" as *konk*. "The Bahamian people," he went on, "believe conch stirs up the libido, making for"—the man paused, displaying a toothy white smile—"very sensual affairs of the heart."

"My companion is so beautiful, I don't think I need any conch tonight," Jake told him.

The waiter agreed that the lady was indeed very lovely, but maintained that a little *konk* would still make things very nice indeed.

As soon as he left with their drink orders, Nila looked at Jake and burst out laughing. "Poor man," she said. "He looked so disappointed when you didn't take his advice."

"Beware the dreaded conch." Jake grinned. "Every establishment on the island pushes conch fritters, conch chowder, conch salad, conch burgers, conch everything but dessert. It doesn't taste too bad, but it's chewier than old leather. I can't imagine why they think it's an aphrodisiac."

"It doesn't sound very appetizing," she agreed.

Tilting her head back, she relaxed and closed her eyes. The music, the sound of the wind rustling through the palm trees, and the scent of exotic flowers filled her senses. If she lived to be a hundred, she knew she would never forget this night. It was a fantasy come true, and a part of her wanted it to go on forever.

She opened her eyes and smiled at Jake. "It's nice out here."

"Would you like to dance?" He rose abruptly and came to stand beside her. "I'm not very good at it, but I'm willing to give it a try."

Nila barely had time to shrug out of his jacket before she was whisked onto the dance floor and into his arms.

"You move faster than a striking snake," she murmured in a good-natured protest.

"Sorry."

"You don't sound at all apologetic."

"You're right. I'm not." He brushed the lightest of kisses against her temple. "I couldn't wait to hold you in my arms. Dancing with you seemed the most expedient method."

Nila sighed. He was, she decided, a man who was overwhelmingly confident with the knowledge that he knew what he wanted and how to get it. Because of her own insecurities, she found that quality very appealing.

They were pressed close together on the jammed wooden floor, and she loosely clasped her hands behind his neck. They fit well together, she thought dreamily. Dangerously well.

Far from being a bad dancer, he moved with fluid ease. She was aware of every sensual movement of his body. A thrust of his hip, the tantalizing brush of his thigh against her pelvis, the warmth of his hands locked firmly and possessively in the center of her back.

As her head found a natural place against his chest, Jake felt his heart beat with the sexy rhythm of the music. Holding her was a drug that entered his bloodstream in a powerful rush. He breathed in deeply, trying to control another sudden surge of desire.

The gentle touch of her fingers at his nape was almost his undoing. A low groan from him brought her head up, and she looked at him questioningly.

Her lips were too close to ignore. With single-minded determination, he seized the opportunity to quench his growing thirst.

Nila's eyes opened wide as his mouth settled firmly, warmly on hers. She hadn't expected him to kiss her. At least, not here. Not now. Not yet. She was unprepared for it, but she couldn't make herself draw away. She was starved for the touch and taste of him.

The demanding pressure of his mouth forced hers to open. He ravished her with his tongue. She moaned and pressed closer. Her skin felt as if it were burning, and she grew weak with the exquisite magic flowing between them.

It was he who finally pulled away.

For a long moment they stood in a frozen tableau while other couples and the music drifted around them.

"Nila?" He spoke her name in a whisper filled with undisguised passion.

She knew she was being seduced again, and she was completely fascinated by it. She was thirty years old, and she had never experienced anything that came remotely close to this.

She sighed. "This is crazy. This isn't real. You're not real. I made you up in my imagination. Maybe I'm hallucinating. What do they put in those sneaky Bahama Mama drinks besides fruit juice?"

He chuckled as he feathered kisses across her forehead. "Coconut rum, dark rum, Nassau Royal. Don't blame this on the one drink you've had. You're not hammered enough to hallucinate, my Bahama Mama. I promise you I'm very real."

She laughed and laid her head on his shoulder. She was glad he was holding her, because she felt dizzy enough to have consumed a dozen sneaky rum concoctions. The night had taken on an accelerated pace. Everything seemed to be moving so fast, and she wasn't sure she could keep up.

The band played the last note of music, and the crowd around them began to disperse. They kept dancing, more swaying back and forth than really moving.

After a moment she murmured, "The music stopped."

"It has?"

"Yes. We should go back to our table now."

"If you want to."

She didn't want to. But it was the thing to do. Reluctantly, she lowered her arms and pulled away.

When they reached their table, Jake threw some

money down for the drinks. "I really don't want to sit here, do you?"

Looking at him through a haze of desire, she couldn't speak, couldn't think rationally. All she knew was that she wanted this man in a way she had never known before. Wordlessly, she picked up her purse and bucket of quarters.

Jake once again draped his jacket over her shoulders, then pinned her securely to his side with his arm around her waist. Without a word, he guided her away from the bar and out to the walkway leading to the guest buildings.

A taut, sensual silence dispatched the tranquility of the Bahamian night. It engulfed Nila until she felt as though her head were spinning faster than a roulette wheel. The air that had seemed so cool upon her skin became heated, heavy.

It only took a few minutes for them to reach the building where Jake had a corner room on the ground floor. But by the time he turned the key in the lock, the tension building in Nila was almost more than she could bear.

He opened the door and switched on a light. Her legs shook as she walked inside. He followed her.

As soon as the door closed, panic attacked her. She had spent her life being a *good* girl, always doing the proper thing, always behaving in a socially correct manner.

Good girls didn't allow themselves to be seduced by sexy, wicked-looking men. What in the world was she getting herself into?

She clung to her evening bag and the plastic bucket. "It's just like my room," she said lamely.

Jake suppressed a grin. He stood with his back against the door, watching her look at everything but him. "A bed, a dresser, table and chairs. Bright tropical colors," he said.

She met his gaze, and he saw by the pink staining her cheeks that she was embarrassed. Poor darling, he thought, dressed up like a good-time girl and acting like she didn't have the faintest idea how to go about having one.

Sweet, that was what she was. Sweet and totally refreshing to a cynical old soul such as himself.

He moved toward her. Stopping within arm's length, he removed the thong binding his hair. He saw her eyes widen as though she was afraid he was going to grab her and tie her up with the thin strip of leather. He tossed the thong onto the dresser.

"Are you all right?" he asked.

"Fine. Just fine," she chirped. She was terrified. She was fascinated. With his black hair swinging free, he looked magnificent and appealingly dangerous, a dark angel ready to fulfill all her fantasies. Taking a walk on the wild side wasn't as easy as it seemed.

He studied her with his intense dark eyes. "You look like you're strung tighter than a guitar string. Relax, sweetheart."

She felt the pull of his attraction, the yearning for a blazing, glorious moment of freedom. That powerful yearning kept her from bolting out the door. But even though she wanted him desperately, her insecurity over her own sexuality kept her from throwing herself into his arms.

"Nila." Her name was a regretful sigh upon his lips. "I've never wanted a woman more than I want you. But if you don't want this as much as I do, then . . ." He hesitated, as though he wasn't quite sure what to say to reassure her. For some reason, she found that small gesture reassuring.

He met her gaze again and smiled. "Look, sweetheart, I promised you'd be as safe as you want to be with me. It's okay if you've changed your mind. I don't want you to leave, but what you want is more important. It's your decision. I don't want to scare you, Nila, but do I? Is that what's wrong?"

Three

Jake's gaze was so piercing, Nila believed he could see the doubts in her practical mind and the secret longings in her heart. She laughed shakily. "No, you don't scare me. I scare myself. I've never done anything like this before. I mean, I'm not a thirty-year-old virgin or anything." She flushed to the roots of her hair. "I guess what I'm trying to say is that I'm not good at this sort of thing. I'm not very brave and I—"

He touched her, stopping her rapid outpouring of words. He cradled her face between his hands and stroked her cheeks with his thumbs. "You're a beautiful, sexy woman and you're doing fine, sweetheart."

A wave of desire curled inside her, starting in the core of her femininity and swirling through her body until it consumed her. She felt weak, helpless, strong, and daring all at the same time. Could this be what women throughout the ages experienced when they encountered a unique man who made them feel beautiful, wanted, and passionately alive?

A laugh bubbled up in her throat and broke free. For the first time in her life, she understood her mother's and sister's obsession with wild, reckless men.

He smiled, a slow, sensual smile. "When you laugh, I don't feel like we're strangers, Nila. When you touch me, I feel we've known each other forever. I need you. I need you for something more than sex. Don't ask me to explain what that something more is, because I can't explain it even to myself."

His words filled her mind and her senses. A new spark ignited inside her, creating a tiny flame that yearned to grow brighter, stronger.

When she finally spoke, her voice was barely audible. "I want to stay with you."

"Then we don't need this, do we?" He took the plastic container holding her casino winnings. "Or this." He removed her satin clutch bag from her loose grip. Turning, he placed them both on the dresser behind him.

When he faced her again, he gazed at her for a long moment, and she realized she was holding her breath. In slow motion he raised his hand and rubbed his knuckles over the top curve of her breasts. She closed her eyes, wanting to press against him, wanting to absorb his strength, his daring and self-assurance, wanting all the qualities so lacking in herself.

"When I went to the casino tonight," he said, "I never dreamed I'd be lucky enough to find you."

She opened her eyes as he slipped his jacket off her shoulders. "I didn't go there intending for anything like this to happen. I wasn't looking for a man."

"I know. I wasn't looking for a woman either." His voice was a tender murmur. "But we found each other. That's all that matters." He showered soft kisses across the bridge of her nose as he pulled her close.

She let him take her mouth, her arms sliding up around his shoulders. She held on to him tightly. Other men had kissed her, but never like this, never as if they were dying and only she could save them.

Rockets exploded inside her, and her fiery reaction shocked her. She'd always kept her passion on a tight leash. Now it threatened to rage out of her control. She wanted to surrender and not be afraid to lose herself in her own sexuality.

"Jake," she whispered as he freed her mouth and kissed a scorching trail to her ear. Her hands slid across his wide shoulders, then she plunged her fingers into his inviting, unbound hair, glorying in its silkiness.

His tongue found the sensitive inner fold of her ear. A shudder passed through his body and was echoed in hers. "We are going to be so good together." He slid his hands over her buttocks, lifting and pressing her boldly into his hips. "Don't think about anything but us and the way we make each other feel."

She couldn't think of anything but the way he made her feel. No longer could she hold herself in check. No longer did she feel the need to be the good girl. No longer did she want to be the sensible, respectable one in the Shepherd family.

She heard her voice as if it belonged to someone else, crying out a low moan. Grabbing fistfuls of his long, bad-boy's hair, she rubbed it against her lips, wanting to taste it, feel it, devour it, as she wanted to devour him and his fearless passion.

With a wicked laugh he swept his hands up her back to capture her head. His mouth closed over hers in a hot kiss that made her legs weak and her heart pound harder than a Bahamian drum.

Then he was pulling the bodice of her dress farther down her shoulders, so that she had to release his hair and lower her arms. She reached for his waist and clutched his hard body to keep from falling.

"I want to see you, touch you," he murmured thickly, rubbing his thumbs over her taut nipples.

Her hands rushed to his belt and frantically unbuckled it. She struggled with his zipper, feeling the hardness of his arousal through his trousers. "I need— I need—"

He raised his head and sucked in his breath. Exhaling long and slow, he said, "I'll give you anything you need and everything you ever dreamed of."

"Will you, Jake?" She lifted her trembling fingers to his tie and began pulling at the knot.

"Yes. Ask and whatever you want is yours."

The snap fastening the green satin bow to the back of her dress gave way beneath his clever fingers. He located the short zipper in the black velvet. Cool air feathered her skin, then was replaced by the warmth of his hands. She whimpered and sought his mouth while she tore at his shirt buttons.

Wild, frenzied, they stripped off each other's clothing. His shirt and tie flew to the floor along with her dress and black lace demibra. He kicked off his shoes, then peeled off socks, trousers, and briefs.

She braced her hands on his shoulders when he knelt down and removed her three-inch heels. His palms traveled slowly up the length of her legs, and ripples of excitement cascaded through her. "Please, Jake," she begged. "Please hurry."

He managed a husky growl of a laugh. "We have all night." He hooked his thumbs in the lacy bands of her thigh-high silk stockings and drew them downward.

"You're perfect," he told her. "Perfect in every way." He kissed the delta of her femininity through her bikini panties before stripping them off. Then he rose up to take her in his arms.

For timeless moment they stared at each other. Hunger along with something unbearably wild shimmered in her gaze and was answered in his, and then he kissed her.

She gave herself up completely to the pleasure of his exploration. Her hips moved sensually to and fro, loving the aroused manhood pressing insistently against her. His hair-roughened thigh thrust between her legs and rubbed the heart of her desire. Her body responded with a quiver of longing, and she dug her nails into his back as she tore her mouth from his and daringly nipped at his shoulders.

Jake groaned and slipped his hands down to explore the secrets hidden by her dark triangle of curls. "You're killing me. You smell so good," he said, breathing in the subtle scent of her perfumed skin.

"Jasmine. It's called Island Promises." Her tongue played with his earlobe. "Made here on the island. Body heat diffuses it," she whispered just before taking his ruby into her mouth.

"And it drives men crazy," he finished for her. He moved his head and his hard, warm mouth settled over hers.

She accepted his tongue and gave him her own in a deep, aggressive kiss that would have made her blush if she had stopped to consider what she was doing. It felt so right to be kissing him, so wonderful to be in this dangerous man's embrace. Oh yes, she thought while wrapping her leg around his, she was absolutely right to take this walk on the wild side with him.

Jake slid his hands up over her waist, over her breasts, then cupped her face. Such an ethereal face, he thought. As he looked deep into her beautiful eyes, so filled with trusting desire, he realized once again that she wasn't a woman to casually bed and forget. She was home and hearth. Someone who needed to be cherished.

Home, hearth, cherish. Those were things he never allowed himself to think about. They were not suited to the life he'd lived.

His breath was unsteady as he forced air in and out of his lungs. "I've done some crazy things in my life, but I think this may be the craziest. God, I want you."

He bent to kiss her throat. "How can anyone feel so good?" The silkiness of her skin and the scent clinging to her filled his senses like the first taste of something new, something rare and delicious.

Nila closed her eyes, waiting in agony to feel his mouth on her breasts. When he lingered too long in the valley between them, lavishing her skin with the tip of his tongue, she groaned in frustration. Threading her fingers through his hair, she guided him to the ache he was creating in her.

His tongue stroked her nipple. She cried out, arching her back to press closer to him. As he gave her what she wanted, she felt something warm and wonderful opening inside her, and she wanted to weep for joy.

When he lifted his head, they were both breathless and shaking. Gathering her to him, he tumbled her back onto the bed. They rolled over and over, his hair raining down over her face, her legs tangled with his, until they hovered precariously on the edge of the king-sized bed. Then they tumbled over.

Breath left Nila's body as her back hit the carpeted floor and Jake sprawled on top of her. For a moment, she was too stunned to move.

"My God, did I hurt you?" He pushed himself up on his knees and raised her off the floor to a sitting position. His arms cradled her in a tender embrace. "I'm so sorry, sweetheart. Are you all right?"

Nila's hands hovered uncertainly over his shoulders. The absurdity of the situation got to her, and a giggle rose in her throat. Her lips trembled with suppressed laughter. "Maybe this is a good time to discuss safe sex," she said in a choked voice, and burst out laughing.

She saw the corners of his mouth turn up, then the sound of his full-hearted laughter joined hers. She rocked back and forth with him, loving the feel of his arms around her, awed by the sensation of closeness created by the unexpected humor.

Jake couldn't pinpoint the exact moment when their shared amusement ignited back into passion. One second he was laughing so hard he thought his lungs would explode, and the next he was shuddering at the feel of her soft breasts crushed against his chest. His hands flowed downward to caress her silky legs, then traveled between her parted thighs.

"Nila, sweet Nila," he groaned as he discovered the evidence of her renewed desire. "You have nothing to fear. You'll be safe with me. I'll take good care of you."

She moaned softly in reply. She couldn't speak. She couldn't think clearly. She could only feel the miracle he worked with his clever fingers as wave after wave of excitement rushed through her body.

Her nails sank into the skin of his shoulders and she cried out his name. Shutting her eyes, she lifted her mouth toward his.

He groaned again and caught her wrists. "Not yet, sweetheart. I have to take care of the future."

Her eyes snapped open. "Future?"

He smiled crookedly. Humor danced like tiny lights in his dark eyes. "You reminded me of it a minute ago. I've taken risks all my life. Deadly risks." His lips touched hers so lightly, she could barely feel them. "But I would never risk your safety. I think you deserve a better man than I. But I swear you'll never regret giving yourself to me."

Nila knew she was flushing vividly. A blatant hunger glittered in his gaze, but he was trying to control it for her sake. The wonder of it brought a radiant smile to her lips.

"It's going to be all right," Jake whispered as he stared into her eyes, trying to absorb in his tired soul all of the gentleness and goodness he saw in them. He kissed her eyelids.

Need twisted inside him. He had known need before, but this was different. It was a new, uncharted, complex sensation, and it created a searing ache through him.

He murmured her name as he raised them both to their feet. Slowly, deliberately he lowered her to the bed. She grasped his arms, trying to drag him down with her. He pried her hands away and clasped them between his own. "I have to take care of you. I promised."

She shook her head. "You are taking care of me. You're loving me." She didn't want him to leave her for even a minute. Her breasts throbbed, anticipating his touch. She wanted more of him and she wanted it now.

"Kiss me, Jake." She pulled one hand free and touched his cheek. "Kiss me again." He obeyed, brushing his lips against hers. She could have wept when he raised his head and stepped back.

"I want you so badly I can taste it." Jake took another step back, stunned by the truth of what he'd said. "I don't dare touch you again until I can make it right for you."

Reluctantly, he left and went into the bathroom, where he rummaged in the basket of toiletries provided by the hotel. It seemed to take him forever to open the foil packet. He swore silently in irritation, unusually awkward with the familiar form of protection. When he finally got it right, he felt like whooping with triumph.

Going back into the bedroom, he stood by the bed and looked down at her. His gaze traveled over her face, then her body, as he memorized every inch of her. Her nipples grew hard under his scrutiny. He bent forward and kissed the satin plane of her stomach.

Nila gave a little sob of frustration. Her hands knotted the bed linens as she twisted and shivered beneath the sweet administration of his mouth. He was unlike any other man in the world, she thought as an inferno of desire blazed inside her.

Eager to please and satisfy in return, she let go of the coverlet and urged him down beside her. His hard arousal pressed against her hip, and her own body responded with a quiver she felt deep within her femininity. She explored the contours of his muscular chest with her fingers, loving the smoothness of his bronzed skin.

Jake whispered her name against the hollow of her throat. He wove his fingers through her hair, loving the way it felt entwined in his hands. Loosening the thin black velvet ribbon that anchored the silky mass in place, he stripped it off and tossed it away.

As he pushed her onto her back, the blood roared so loudly in his ears, he was surprised she couldn't hear it. He knew he had hustled her into spending time with him at the casino. He knew he had seduced her into his bed. As he found the taut peak of her breast with his tongue and his lips, he vowed he would never give her reason to regret this night.

He began to murmur his need for her, and his words sounded like sonnets to Nila. As he spoke of how she made him feel, he kissed a trail from her breasts to the core of her heated desire. Again and again, she moaned beneath his exquisite touch and his incredibly erotic words, which would have been shocking coming from anyone but him.

She splayed her legs and felt his long hair brush against the sensitive skin of her inner thighs. Never had she felt so primitive, so completely free. She trembled violently as the tension in her body raged out of control. Then something wonderful, something indescribable exploded inside her, and she arched her hips off the bed.

"Jake!" she cried out in glorious release.

She had barely finished calling his name before he shifted and she felt the impact of his weight upon her body. Her head spun faster than a roulette wheel as he plunged himself between her thighs. She dug her fingers into his back. When she lifted herself to meet him, he stormed her body in an undeniable act of possession that took her breath away.

"All right?" he murmured against her lips.

"Yes. Oh, yes," she cried, wrapping her arms around his back and her legs around his hips. She gave herself up completely to a passion so rich, so sensual, she became crazy with it.

Together, they were lusty and insatiable. They reached a perfect tempo that bound them to each other in wave after wave of rapture.

Nila felt herself soaring high toward a peak of ecstasy. She clung to him as tension gripped her quaking body. Fiery sensations rippled through her, then tiny lights flashed behind her tightly closed eyes. A moan of pleasure escaped her lips as he joined her in divine release.

Feeling dazed, she floated down from the clouds of heaven, breathing in deep as he relaxed his body along hers. Their joining was everything she had imagined lovemaking should be. Never had she known anything like this. Never had any man made her feel so fully alive and aware of the power of her own femininity. For the first time in her life, she felt unrestrained joy in her sexuality. It was a gift so astonishing, she could hardly bear it.

He lifted his head from her breast. Cradling her face between his warm hands, he looked down at her with an expression of languid male satisfaction that sent a thrill racing up her spine.

She reached up and brushed a lock of his tangled hair away from his face. "You've made every fantasy I've ever had come true," she said shyly. She would never forget this night or this man. She imagined herself as an old, wrinkled lady smiling to herself as she remembered the dark, passionate angel of her youth.

"This isn't a fantasy. It's real." He feathered a kiss across her lips. "You're mine now," he whispered so softly, she was sure she'd imagined the words.

He took her mouth in a warm, lingering kiss,

then he rolled to one side. "Let's see if the shower is large enough for two."

She yelped in protest as he swept her off the bed and into his arms. He smiled. She was coming to adore his dimple and his shark's smile, she thought, allowing him to carry her into the bathroom.

Half an hour later, after the most erotic shower of her life, Nila found herself back in bed with Jake. For a moment they lay peacefully in each other's arms. Her fingers played across his smooth, still-damp chest. His hand rubbed her arm from elbow to shoulder, creating delicious sensations.

Hearing her sigh of contentment, Jake turned and gazed down at the top of her head, cradled as it was upon his chest. Emotion, unfamiliar and incredibly tender, filled him.

She lifted her head and looked at him. "This is nice, isn't it?"

He felt his body tightening again. "It's amazing." He reached over to the nightstand and prepared himself again, more expertly than the first time. "And it's getting more amazing by the minute," he growled as he rolled over to trap her body beneath his. Gazing into her eyes, he entered her aggressively, possessing her and filling her with all the emotion with which she had filled him.

This time their joining was more ferocious and untamed than before. And when their passion was spent, they lay damp and wonderfully replete in each other's arms.

Feeling like a weary traveler who had finally reached his destination, Jake moved onto his side and pulled her back against him in a loose embrace. His mind conjured up plans for himself and the sweet lady who made his jaded soul feel new again. "Tomorrow we'll go snorkeling."

"I've never done that before."

"The reefs are spectacular. You'll love it. The marine life is unlike anything you've ever seen. Jewels below the sea in all the finest colors you can imagine." He smiled and kissed her hair. "We'll go shopping at the International Bazaar. We'll take a sunset cruise around the island." His eyes drifted closed, and he held her as he slept.

Nila awoke with a start. Her foggy brain registered the heavy feel of a masculine arm draped over her breasts. She lay very still for a moment. Finally dredging up more courage than she'd ever given herself credit for, she forced her eyes open. Stark morning light streaked in through a small slit in the curtains and danced around the room.

She turned her face and stared at the dark head sharing the pillow with her. Only a monumental effort kept her from gasping aloud.

Jake! The aggressive lines of his face were softened in his sleep. A sunbeam made the ruby in his earlobe sparkle wickedly. Her gaze traveled from his tangled black hair to his massive shoulder, coming to rest upon the sinewy arm that pinned her to the bed.

She swallowed as she remembered the indelible imprint he had left upon her physically and emotionally the night before. The enormity of what she had done made her cringe. Bleakly she wondered which shocked her more: that she had gone to bed with a man she barely knew, or that she was more than half in love with him.

Fear whispered through her as she thought of the way she had become a wild woman in his arms. Why had she been so foolish? For a moment she hated herself, hated him. She had only herself to blame, she thought savagely. Feeling a wave of nausea, she closed her eyes and wondered how she was going to get out of this mess.

Holding her breath, she gently put her hand on his arm. He murmured something but remained asleep. Lifting his arm, she eased away from him. Slowly she inched over to the edge of the bed and got up.

She gathered her clothes and dressed quickly, praying all the while that he wouldn't wake up. She didn't want him to open his eyes and discover that the woman who had responded with such abandon to him last night was really a poor-spirited creature, filled with a quivering mass of insecurities.

At the door, she paused and glanced back at him. For a second her fear was replaced by a terrible longing that made her heart twist painfully. She smiled sadly, then blew a silent kiss of good-bye to her glorious fantasy.

Jake's internal alarm woke him. Several realizations hit him at once. First, Nila was no longer curled up beside him. Second, he'd slept peacefully without being tortured by the nightmare that usually had him waking up in a cold sweat. Third, the bed felt unbearably empty. The significance of the last two thoughts made him jackknife up to a sitting position.

His gaze traveled over the room. Her clothes were gone. Nila was gone!

An irrational shock held him frozen. It had barely passed before his gaze locked upon the only thing she'd lift behind. Looking at the container sporting the colorful Bahamas Queen Casino logo, he felt as though he'd been punched in the face.

She'd left her winnings sitting on the dresser like payment for a night's pleasure.

Anger and a sense of indignation ate at him. He could almost feel his blood bubbling through his veins.

"No!" The single word exploded from his throat and echoed in his mind. It hadn't been like that. Not for him. Not for her. It had been much more than a simple night's pleasure.

He reached for the phone, pressed zero, then asked the hotel operator to ring Nila's room. A minute later he hung up after being told Ms. Shepherd had checked out half an hour ago.

Hurt replaced anger and indignation. He sat down on the edge of the bed, braced his arms on his knees, and stared at the floor. He had no doubt she was on her way to the airport. Even if he left now, he probably wouldn't catch her in time.

Why had she run? She had given herself willingly and completely to him last night. Didn't she understand she belonged to him now?

He wanted to break something. His gaze was drawn to the bucket of coins. He wanted to pick it up and throw it through the window. Fighting a fresh wave of anger, he balled his hands into fists, then rose and began to pace.

He needed her. Needed her sweetness and passion. Needed the decency he'd seen in her beautifully soft eyes.

She kept the nightmare away.

He closed his eyes as a heavy, sick feeling settled in the pit of his stomach. His legs turned to water. No one, not even his ex-partner, knew how close he had come to crossing over the edge. No one knew how he relived in his dreams the horror of what had almost happened in the back room of a seedy bar in Miami.

Nila kept the nightmare away.

Determination tightened his jaw. Jake sat down on the bed again, grabbed the phone, and punched in a number. "Come on, Rae, answer," he muttered impatiently as he listened to it ring. "Amazon, it's me," he said when a woman finally answered.

"Mad Man? Where the hell are you? What time is it?"

He smiled with affection at the sleepy, out-of-sorts tone of his former partner's voice. "Eight o'clock," he said, glancing at the clock. "I'm in Freeport. What's the matter? You been out chasing bad guys all night?"

"The baddest of the bad, baby." Her silvery laugh filled Jake's ear. "Are you calling for a reason, or are you just missing me?"

"Why would I miss you, you ugly amazon?" His smile broadened. There was nothing ugly or amazonlike about Rae Garcia. Half Irish, half Cuban, she was a five-foot-five-inch beauty with sooty eyes that had caused more than one criminal's heart to do back flips as he grudgingly spilled his guts. "I need some information, quick."

"Are you onto something there?" She sounded instantly alert. "I thought you retired," she added as an afterthought.

"I am retired. It's personal. I need you to dig up everything you can about a woman named Nila Shepherd. The only thing I know is she lives in a small town called Danville in Virginia."

Rae didn't speak for a long moment. "Personal? Why don't you just ask her what you want to know?"

He ran his hand over his face. Feeling extremely idiotic, he said, "I would, but I can't. She took off on me this morning. I don't even know her address or what she does for a living."

Sudden quiet, then an eruption of laughter. "Mad Man, you must be losing your touch. What'd you do, scare her off?" She made a few disparaging remarks about his manhood in raunchy street Spanish.

Jake sighed in frustration. "Just find out what you can." He rattled off the hotel phone number, then hung up with Rae's laughter still ringing in his ears.

Four

Nila arrived back in Danville early Sunday evening. The panic that had driven her to flee the Bahamas that morning had faded, leaving her feeling foolish and disgusted with herself.

She sighed with relief as she unlocked the door of her Victorian house. Never had home looked so welcoming, so safe. She ignored the correspondence and the phone messages that had piled up during her short absence, too drained and shaky to deal with them. All she wanted to do was crawl into bed and sleep away her shame and humiliation.

An hour later, she emerged from a long, hot shower, worn out from a crying jag. She took out a clean white nightgown and shrugged into it.

In bed with the linens pulled up to her chin, she focused on her reflection in the cheval mirror. No hint remained of the wild woman she'd become in Jake's arms. Her eyes, huge as the eyes of an urchin in a Save This Child picture, were red and swollen. She wished the pitiful thing looking back at her was someone else.

"A one-night stand," she muttered, squeezing her eyes shut. It sounded so sleazy! How could she have allowed herself to become so intimately involved with a stranger? How could she have behaved so stupidly? How could she have kissed her morals and good sense good-bye so easily?

Her mind had been stuck on that same horrible litany since she'd left Jake asleep in his hotel room. The answers she kept coming up with were not comforting.

She couldn't deceive herself into believing Jake had taken advantage of her. He hadn't pressured her into doing anything she hadn't wanted to do. She knew he would have respected a firm no. Lord help her, but she'd wanted to be wild with him. He had only fulfilled her secret need to feel beautiful, sexy, outrageous, and desirable.

It had seemed so right at the time. They had been two people who had recognized each other as lonely kindred spirits. Yet that didn't alter the disgraceful facts in the least. It had been a terrible mistake. She had simply allowed her foolish fantasy to go too far.

If she had stayed with him, she greatly feared she would have offered him her heart and soul along with her body. Having witnessed her mother's and sister's frequent heartbreaks, Nila knew she could not bear to take such an emotional risk.

She turned off the bedside lamp. Lying in the darkness, she couldn't help wondering how Jake was feeling. Most likely, she had merely been a brief encounter to him, a vacation fling. He'd probably woken up that morning and thanked his lucky stars to find himself alone.

Nila sighed. The sound was webbed with misery.

• • •

Monday morning Nila forced herself to get out of bed, get dressed, and go downstairs to open her combination book, gift, and gourmet food store.

The first thing Angie Parker, her best friend and employee, said to her when she arrived a few minutes later was, "What the hell are you doing here? You're supposed to be sunning your buns in the Bahamas."

"I was homesick," Nila answered morosely from her perch on a padded stool behind the cash register. She had made up her mind the night before never to tell anyone what had happened between herself and Jake Madison.

"Bull dooty." Angie dumped her purse down on the counter. "I made your reservation at the best resort. I loaned you my clothes. You owe me an explanation." She fished around inside her purse and came up with a gold cigarette case and lighter. She fired one up.

Nila handed her the crystal ashtray she kept under the counter. "I thought you were quitting."

"I am." She took a deep drag. "I'm down to three a day. Breakfast, lunch, and dinner. Finding you` here has upset my schedule."

"That's a pathetic excuse."

"And your excuse is thinner than a politician's campaign promise."

Nila sighed. "Paradise is a lonely place when you're alone." A chill went up her spine as she realized she'd quoted Jake.

"Oh, hon!" Angie's baby blue eyes filled with concern. She stubbed out her cigarette and reached for Nila's hand. "I should have gone with you. I had hoped you'd find some handsome little honey who could . . . I'm sorry, Nila."

Nila felt guilty for an instant. Still, she didn't want to tell even her oldest and dearest friend what a fool she'd made of herself. She smiled and squeezed Angie's hand. "Don't be sorry. You couldn't leave Miles. Besides, you're the only one I trust to take care of business in my absence."

The bell above the shop jangled as the door opened. Clover Norville entered with her usual storm-trooper grace. "Nila Ann, what the hell are you doing home?" She stopped to hitch up her red knee socks.

"She was homesick," Angie answered for her. "Good morning, Aunt Clover."

Clover blew a raspberry at her niece and headed for the hot pot over by the display of coffees and teas. "What kind did you make today, Nila?"

"Colombian Armenia Supremo," Nila answered, her gaze riveted to Clover's hat. It looked like an inverted pink flower. The ancient spray of silk violets pinned to the brim dangled rakishly over her brow. "Nice hat," she managed to say with a straight face.

"Don't try to get on my good side, Nila Ann. My good side departed with my second husband. Are you over the bug you had up your butt about that deadhead, Frank Tate?" Clover glanced at Nila over her shoulder as she vigorously stirred raw sugar into her coffee.

Clover was sixty-four and figured she could get away with saying what ever she pleased to anyone she pleased. Most of the time she was right. She had been getting away with it as long as Nila could remember.

Before she could form a reply to Clover's question, Angie jumped to her defense. "Do you have to be so crude and insensitive, Aunt Clover?"

"Hush up, Miss Buttinsky. I wasn't talking to you."

Angie caught her aunt's hard-edged stare and threw it back like a Frisbee. "Can't you see Nila doesn't want to talk about that rat?"

"I just asked her a simple question."

"You're only making matters worse."

Nila let them snipe at each other for a moment while she tried to sort out why she suddenly felt so annoyed. It wasn't Clover's plain speaking. She was used to that. It didn't have anything to do with her ex-fiancé dumping her, either. She was annoyed, she realized, because she hadn't been given the chance to speak for herself.

Angie had spoken for her out of habit. Although it had never bothered Nila before, it bothered her now. Since childhood, she had hated confrontations and unpleasantness. So she had always allowed Angie to run interference for her and fight her battles.

She wasn't sure where the need to fight her own battles was coming from, but she looked upon it as a positive sign of personal growth. It was time she stopped being such a wimp.

Gathering her courage, she took her first step toward cutting the dependent cord that tied her to Angie's apron string. "Stop it! I've had just about enough out of both of you."

The two women went silent and looked at her— Clover with amazement and Angie with hurt.

"I love you," Nila told Angie, softening the blow of her bid for independence. "But I can speak for myself." She smiled at her and received a surprised but supportive one in return.

To them both she said, "I don't still have a bug up my butt about Frank. He can elope with a dozen secretaries for all I care. Our engagement was a mistake. I didn't like being dumped, but my heart isn't broken." Though her newfound courage was rapidly running out of gas, she forced herself to add, "Now, dammit, the subject is closed."

"Well, good," Clover said. "I'm impressed with your change in attitude." She took her coffee over to a chair and flopped down. "Men are the most horrible creatures on earth. They'll spend your money and ruin your life. I've told your mama and sister that a thousand times. Emma and Mary are so dumb about men, they just keep on reaching into the barrel and picking out the rotten ones. You have better sense than that, I know."

Nila squirmed uncomfortably. No, she didn't. She'd picked the safest, most predictable bachelor banker in town to become engaged to, and he'd dumped her for a woman with Dolly Parton boobs. So then she'd run off to the Bahamas with her wounded pride and hopped into bed with the first handsome devil to ask her.

Clover's sharp voice dragged her from glum thoughts. "Angie Parker, your fanny is practically showing." Clover critically eyed Angie's black dancer's tights, suede boots, and sweater that barely reached the tops of her thighs. "I'd be embarrassed to wear something like that in public."

"At least *I* have a unique sense of style. You should be embarrassed to wear that hat in public."

"It's my dead sister's hat! Coralie knew more about style than your fluff-bunny brain will ever know."

Angie ran her fingers through her Nordic blond hair and gave Nila a long-suffering look. "Aunt Coralie has been dead for twenty years." She addressed Clover. "That hat is deader than Aunt Coralie."

"Is not!" Clover said indignantly.

"Is too," Angie shot back. "Give it a decent burial."

Nila shook her head and let them go at it. She loved them both, but sometimes, they just plain wore her out. Life had a way of taking on the absurd quality of a situation comedy when they were around.

She put on her tortoiseshell glasses and went to work on her Christmas-season gourmet food order.

By mid-morning the word was out that Nila was back, and customers flocked in to express their shock and sympathy over Frank Tate's scandalous behavior. They went through two pots of Colombian Armenia Supremo and one pot of raspberry tea while they sang the praises of various unmarried sons, brothers, male cousins, or nephews. When Nila politely declined to be fixed up with any of those paragons of virtue, their conversation moved on to books, recipes, local politics, and Angie Parker's outfit.

The next four days were depressingly the same, until Nila was sick to death of being cast into the role of tragic victim. If she thought she could survive the shocking consequences, she would have taken out an ad in the newspaper proclaiming she'd met the fantasy man of her most secret dreams and it wasn't that deadhead, Frank.

Near the end of her working day on Saturday, she decided her life was in the toilet. She hadn't called in her gourmet food order because her mind seemed more interested in thinking about Jake Madison than in making decisions on Cajun spiced peanuts and Korean hot sauce.

How could she possible miss a man she barely knew? That was the question that was keeping her awake at night and screwing up her decision-making abilities. She kept telling herself he was a mistake and she should forget him. But her heart kept saying, "Fat chance. You left a piece of me with a dark angel in a hotel room on the Grand Bahama Island."

Her mom would be so pleased if she knew her staid younger daughter wasn't quite so straitlaced after all.

At ten minutes to six that evening, Jake Madison watched a tall blonde come out of Nila's shop, Books, Gifts, & Things. As she walked past, she gave his white Mustang convertible a curious glance. The look she gave him was less benign and filled with suspicion.

He returned her gaze with a slight nod. She hurried on across the street to join an older woman who stood in the yard of an impressive home with stained glass windows. Both women glanced in his direction, then exchanged a few words. No doubt they were wondering why he was just sitting in his car and if he was up to no good.

Jake took a deep breath, pulling up the calm, centering himself as he fine-tuned his nerves and studied the scene before committing himself. Rae's report on Nila Shepherd had brought him to this address. She was somewhere inside the house he had been watching for the past fifteen minutes.

The area Nila lived in was called Millionaire's Row and was perched high on a hill overlooking the cobblestone streets of downtown Danville. In a valley between rolling hills was the Dan River and the more modern section of town, jammed with shopping centers and fast-food restaurants.

As far as he could see along the tree-lined street were well-preserved houses that represented a bygone era of architecture and a vanishing way of life. Having driven through the neighborhood several times before parking beside a massive Victorian house, Jake had noticed that many of the grand homes had been converted into shops and law offices.

Against a hazy, multicolored sunset, Nila's place looked like something made out of spun sugar. He knew it was the house she had grown up in, and it had a stately but charming presence, with two distinctive features. One was a wide veranda adorned with detailed work. It wrapped the house from the left side, across the front, and ended in a gazebo on the right. The other, and perhaps more distinctive, feature was a round turret that jutted out from the left front corner of the house, its peak rising above the roofline.

Jake got out and headed for the house. Up on the veranda, he peered through a window and saw a big high-ceilinged room devoted to the books she sold. Beyond it through a double archway was an area of attractively displayed merchandise.

He didn't see anyone in the store, until a woman moved from behind a rack of books and into his line of vision. His gaze passed over her, then instantly returned.

It was Nila. For a split second he hadn't recognized her. She had told him she tiptoed through life. He hadn't realized she meant she hid her beauty and passion behind egghead glasses, baggy pants, and a cable knit sweater better suited to a woman twice her size.

"You can run, Nila," he murmured, smiling,

"but you can't hide who you are from me." Determined to claim the woman who belonged to him, Jake turned toward the entrance.

Nila was standing in the mystery section, finishing Angie's task of shelving new books, when she heard someone come in. "That didn't take long," she called out, thinking it was Angie returning from her mission to coax her six-year-old son out from under Clover's back porch. "Is Miles still protecting the spiders? Or were you able to persuade him to surrender?"

"Hello, Nila." The shockingly familiar voice, infusing the simple greeting with more intimate meaning, slapped the grin off Nila's face.

Icy fingers of disbelief coursed down her spine. The book she held slipped from her hand. Slowly she turned around.

Jake Madison stood blocking the door of her shop like a sentry. The ruby sparkled in its usual place, and he was wearing tight jeans, a black turtleneck jersey, leather bomber jacket, and boots. He appeared even more darkly powerful and bad to the bone than the last time she'd seen him.

A terrible sense of inevitability paralyzed her. She sucked in a breath of air as she struggled with the realization that Jake had tracked her down.

His gaze swept over the shop. Observing, interested, curious. Camera eyes, she thought, taking snapshots and filing them away in his mind. Then those eyes sought and held her gaze. Was there some way, she wondered frantically, to make herself immune to the black silk strands of his hair that invited her touch, to the vivid and heart-stopping memory of a dark angel asleep on rumpled white sheets?

"Why did you run?" He looked at her with such penetrating directness, she felt as though he could see every living cell in her body. "Who were you afraid of? Me?" He smiled. "Or yourself?"

Nila flinched. Her fears were too numerous and too emotionally painful. She couldn't bear thinking about them, much less express them aloud.

"You look shocked to see me," he added.

She opened her mouth to speak. Nothing happened. Why did the room suddenly feel like the inside of a blazing furnace? Hot and cold waves crawled over her skin. Black dots swam in her vision.

"Nila?" The tone he used this time was laced with concern.

She vaguely realized the blur coming toward her was Jake. Her knees buckled. She grabbed for the book cart to steady herself, but it was too late. The floor seemed to be rising up to meet her, she thought just before her mind mercifully shut down.

Jake knelt beside Nila and gathered her into his arms. After days of angry impatience while he waited for information, after days of wondering what state of mind he might find her in . . . This of all her possible reactions was one he hadn't anticipated.

A raw torrent of emotions he barely recognized made him feel light-headed. His gaze traveled over her face, taking in its alarming paleness and the blue-black shadows beneath her eyes. His fingers searched out her pulse, the erratic beating of her heart. He removed her glasses and set them aside, then stroked her hair, pulling clinging strands away from her lips. Desire rose so immediately as his fingertips brushed her mouth, he closed his eyes against the powerful onslaught.

Even as he was telling himself no, he pulled her closer. Aching hunger drove his fingers through her hair. His mouth hovered just above hers, caressing her lips with the warmth of his breath before he slowly brought them together.

Lost in a dreamer's sensuality, lost in a flood of emotions so strange to him, Jake didn't realize someone had entered the shop until it was almost too late. His instincts warned him at the last second, and only his quick reflexes saved him. He lowered Nila to the floor and twisted his body to the left, and the blow meant for the back of his head caught him on the shoulders.

"Get away from her!" screamed a menacing female voice as glass shattered over him.

Jake rolled to his feet while hard pellets scattered on the floor like a rain shower of colorful BBs. Spinning in place, he thrust out his right arm and deflected the punch of a fist with his elbow.

"Pervert!" yelled the blond woman he'd seen leaving the shop. "What did you do to my friend?"

"Nothing." Keeping an eye on the jagged bottleneck in her hand, he flowed backward, his hands up and ready. "She fainted."

"Ha! Lying rapist. I saw you attacking her." She came at him, wild-eyed and furious.

Jake flicked his hand as she rushed him. The bottleneck went flying. The blonde backpedaled as he spun away from her. "I didn't hurt Nila. She—" He shut up and dodged as she fired off a volley of paperbacks.

A book whined past his ear. Another glanced off his chest. "Rapist!" she hissed as a third book just missed slamming into his groin.

That did it. Now he was ticked. He didn't want to hurt this crazy woman, but enough was enough. He wouldn't attack her. He would only complete the circle she had begun.

He folded into a catlike aikido stance, hands

extended, fingertips out. *Ki* to *ki*. All balance centered deep within his abdomen. He stood rooted, keeping his point, fingers in motion as though connected to his hysterical opponent by invisible wires.

The blonde rushed at him again, ready to scratch his eyes out with her talonlike nails.

Nila returned to awareness, disturbed by a hazy memory of making a spectacle of herself by fainting. She felt something lying on her cheek and picked it up.

It was a jelly bean. A red one. Her favorite. She eased up on her elbows. Why was she covered with gourmet jelly beans and bits of glass?

A guttural scream, the sound about as friendly as an angry panther, bought her head up. Horrified, she saw Angie launch herself with murderous intent toward Jake.

He didn't move, then his left hand fluttered, a butterfly motion. In a flash of movement so fast Nila could barely assimilate it, Jake caught Angie's wrist and drove her to her knees.

"Oh! Ouch! Let go, you pervert. You're breaking my wrist."

"Nonsense," he said. "If I wanted to break it, it would be broken. I'm just applying enough pressure to get your attention."

Angie sneered and aimed a fist at the only portion of his anatomy within her reach—his leg.

Jake sidestepped the blow and eyed his assailant as though she were an annoying puppy chewing on his boot. "Watch it, lady. I don't want to hurt you. And I'm not too fond of being called a pervert and a rapist."

"Eat dirt and die!" She took another swipe at him.

"Shut up and listen. I'm Ja—"

"Jake Madison," Nila said in loud but shaky voice.

That got their attention. They both froze for a moment, then Jake released Angie and she jumped to her feet. His gaze bore into Nila's, seeking answers to questions.

Nila sighed wearily. She had danced to the music. Now it was time to pay the fiddler. She straightened her shoulders and held her chin high. She knew she must appear ridiculously defiant and resentful, sitting there on the floor surrounded by thirty flavors of jelly beans, but she couldn't help it. That was the way she felt: ridiculous, defiant, resentful—and backed into a corner by her own foolish behavior.

"Angie Parker, this is Jake Madison. He's the handsome little honey you hoped I'd meet in the Bahamas." Her tone was as polite as a society hostess's introducing guests at a tea party. "Jake, Angie is my best friend. She owns that damn dress that started all this trouble."

Her friend's wide-eyed, startled expression was priceless. She turned to Jake and stammered, "Oh . . . well . . . uh, nice to meet you. Sorry I tried to kill you."

Jake shook Angie's hand. "I loved that dress. I hope I didn't hurt you."

Someday, Nila hoped, she would look back and remember this with great amusement. But at the moment, she didn't find it funny at all.

The shop door suddenly burst open, and Nila felt the blood drain from her face. She had thought things couldn't possibly get any worse. Now she knew the bull dooty had really just hit the fan.

Five

"Police! Nobody move!"

Hollow with disbelief, Nila watched as not one but *four* of Danville's finest boys in blue skidded to a stop inside her shop. Guns! They had guns! Oh Lord, she'd never had a gun pointed at her before.

"Keep your hands away from your body!" an officer yelled. "Raise them above your head!"

Angie was putty colored. Trembling and speechless, she shot her hands up immediately.

A young, freckle-faced cop bounced forward, jerky as a puppet on a string, gun extended at the full reach of both arms. Nila knew him from church. His first name was Billy. Billy *what*? She frantically tried to recall and couldn't.

"Hands, hands!" he screamed at Jake. "Get 'em up."

"I'm not carrying a weapon, officer." Jake extended both arms out and up. Nila could only stare openmouthed at his perfectly calm attitude. Watching him cross his legs and sink down to his knees, she shuddered, thinking he showed an alarming familiarity with the drill.

High-voltage hysteria brought her to her feet. "Stop it! You're making a mistake."

"Now, Ms. Shepherd," Billy said as another officer handcuffed Jake. "Don't you worry about a thing. We've got 'im covered." To Jake he uttered the fateful words. "Bub, you twitch so much as an eyelash and you'll *make my day*."

Nila ignored the young Dirty Harry hopeful and tuned to the policeman frisking Jake for concealed weapons. "Stop this instant. He didn't do anything wrong. Take those handcuffs off him." She resisted Billy's efforts to move her aside, slapping at his hand.

Jake, still infuriatingly calm, said, "It's all right, sweetheart. Let them do their job. Then they'll be ready to talk. We'll get everything straightened out." He grinned at her. "Bet you wished you'd stayed in bed with me in the Bahamas."

The policeman frisking Jake gave Nila a what-did-he-say look. He began reciting the Miranda in an uncertain voice.

Nila bit back a groan and pressed her hands to her flaming cheeks. At the sound of running feet, she whirled around. Her heart sank down to her stomach as Clover Norville rushed in.

"If he tries anything, shoot him in the privates!" the older woman yelled, swinging a baseball bat with the determination of a batter prepared to hit one out of the park.

Nila's shouted, "Watch out!" came too late. The baseball bat connected with a potted plant on the checkout counter. The ceramic pot fell and knocked over a book display left over from Halloween. Dirt, plant, and horror novels went flying in all directions.

That's when Nila lost it. Her shop, her life, her reputation were destroyed. Her legs buckled. She sat down on the floor, put her head between her knees, and laughed hysterically.

In some distant corner of her mind she heard Angie plead, "May I put my hands down now? Does anybody have a cigarette? Please, I *need* a cigarette."

Fifty minutes later, Nila was stretched out on her blue pin-striped sofa. It truly amazed her how fast a life and reputation could go down the toilet. She could hear the cause of her current problems prowling around her sitting room, but she couldn't see him because a damp cloth covered her face.

She still couldn't believe what had happened. It had taken the longest thirty minutes of her life to make the police officers understand the events that had taken place. Jake's former occupation had been revealed during their interrogation, and by the time they left—with much backslapping and guffawing—they seemed to think the whole thing had been a great joke on one of their own. Billy, whose last name Nila still couldn't remember, departed starry-eyed, having solicited Jake's promise that he wouldn't leave town without telling Billy a few stories about his undercover days over a cold brew or two.

It hadn't been as easy to persuade Clover to go home. "Bad company," she had said repeatedly, stroking her baseball bat. "Mark my words, Nila Ann Shepherd, that man is trouble. Just say the word and I'll send him packing with a flea in his ear."

To Nila's relief, Angie had finally taken the bat away from her aunt and herded her out the door.

Nila sighed, knowing she couldn't put off a confrontation with Jake any longer. She uncovered her face and sat up. "All right, Jake. Why are you here?"

"Feeling better now?" he asked, keeping his back to her as he examined an elegant inlaid tea table. It was her favorite piece in the room and she couldn't help but wonder what he thought of it.

"I'll live. Why are you here?"

He didn't answer as he crossed the Oriental rug to stand in front of the fireplace. His gaze slowly traveled over the family photographs littering the mantel. "Is this your mother and sister?" He picked up a silver-framed picture. "You're the little girl in the pink dress? How old were you?"

She remembered all too well the day that photograph had been taken. "Yes. That's my mother, Emma, and my sister, Mary. I was seven. Mary was twelve. It was Easter and Mama made me wear that dress. I felt silly in all those pink and white ruffles and that big satin bow in my hair."

He flashed her a bone-melting smile. "I wish I had known you then. You look so pretty and sweet. I see that beauty is a family trait."

Nila's eyes widened. She was used to such comments as, "Your mother looks young enough to be your sister," or "Mary looks just like your beautiful mother. You must favor your father." She wasn't used to being included in the admiration of her family's good looks.

"You said Emma and Mary don't live in Danville anymore?" he said.

"No. Mama's third husband built her a new house here in town." She hesitated, waiting for the reaction her mother's marital track record usually incurred. He didn't so much as lift an eyebrow.

"Mama kept the house after her husband died, but she isn't there very often. She's spending the winter in Arizona with a friend." A male friend.

"Mary has lived in Boston since her first marriage."

"Why aren't you smiling in this picture?" he asked, returning the photograph to the mantel. "Is it because you didn't like your dress?"

"No." She gave him points for his nonjudgmental attitude toward her family. "I wasn't smiling because I missed my dad." He walked toward her, and she resented the sudden flutter of her heart. "He left us just before that photograph was taken."

"I'm sorry." He sank down on the opposite end of the sofa from her. "It must have been a hard time for you."

His compassion made Nila uncomfortable. She rarely talked about her father. She didn't know why she'd told Jake even that much. "There's no need to be sorry. It's ancient history."

His eternally watchful gaze roved over her face. "Ancient but not forgotten, I think. It still hurts, doesn't it?"

"I'd rather not discuss it." She curled up into the corner, resting her arms on her knees and lowering her chin to her forearm to stare broodingly at him. "Why are you here?"

"That question is beginning to sound like a broken record."

"And you still haven't given me an answer."

"It should be obvious." He smiled.

Nila felt a little weak at the sight of his adorable dimple. She closed her eyes, fighting the sensual memory of exploring it with her tongue. Looking at him again, she tried to read his thoughts. As usual, she couldn't. Had his line of work taught him to distance himself? Or had he been good at his job because it was his nature to be distant?

"It may be obvious to you, but it isn't to me."

She pushed up her sleeves and primly folded her hands.

"I've come to claim what's mine." His dark eyes glittered dangerously. "I told you before you went to sleep in my arms that you belonged to me."

"Jake! You can't mean that," she whispered. The tension level in the room rose alarmingly. "What happened between us was a mistake. I was upset because my fiancé had just married another woman."

His expression hardened. "Did you love him?"

"No," she said flatly.

"Then don't drag another man into this, Nila. There were no ghosts sharing our bed that night. Why did you leave like that?"

"Because I couldn't face the complications," she said heatedly. "I was mortified by what I had done. You were my first and *last* one-night stand." Her face burned with shame.

"No! It wasn't a one-night stand. It was more than that and you know it."

On his feet again, he stared down at her, frustration evident in every line of his lean, hard body. "That's the real reason you left, isn't it?"

"Jake!" she exclaimed when he reached down to pull her up.

"Look me in the eye and tell me the truth." He grasped her by the shoulders, his fingers digging into the nubby weave of her sweater. "Do you really think what happened between us was a cheap one-night stand?"

Nila heard his words, but it was his voice she felt. It caressed her skin, stimulated her nerve endings, and winged its way into her heart. Her will dissolved like airborne carbonated bubbles. It wasn't fair. How could he do that to her so easily?

"Yes, it was a one-night stand," she said, trying

to put conviction into her words, trying to believe them for all she was worth.

"Wrong answer."

She raised her hands in a useless attempt to stop him as he encircled her with his arms. Her palms flattened against his chest, and she could feel his tightly curving muscles and the steady rhythm of his heart. Inside herself she felt the stir of the wild, passionate woman only he could free.

One of his hands burned a trail over her back to the rounded curve of her buttocks, then sloping under, he eased her up on her toes. "I would have followed you home the day you left, but you didn't leave a forwarding address."

"How did you find me?" she whispered, feeling the stir, the ache of desire.

"I used my DEA connections. I would have been here sooner, but I was called back to Miami to testify against a drug dealer I arrested months ago."

His head bent toward her, and she could feel his warm mouth seeking hers. She murmured a protest, but it was only a token one. His mouth searched over her trembling lips, increasing the pressure until she was dragged into a deep kiss that was long, hard, and rapturous.

After a moment, the kiss wandered across her cheek. Nila might have been made from gelatin for all the strength left in her body. If he hadn't been holding her up, surely she would have slithered to the floor.

With effort she dredged up her waning ability to reason. "Jake, you don't understand. The woman you met that night isn't the real me. I'm not like that at all."

"Not like what?" His breath teased her earlobe

just before the tip of his tongue began to explore the sensitive inner chamber of her ear.

Her mind whirled with momentary dizziness. She snaked her arms up to his shoulders and held on to him tightly. "Passionate. Reckless. Free."

He lifted his head. Catching her chin in his hand, he smiled down at her. "Yes you are. You've just been hiding it behind egghead glasses and baggy clothes. All you needed was the right man to set that part of you free. That man is me. We're paper and fire. I know you feel it."

"What do you want from me?" It was a desperate plea. She shut her eyes, wishing she could stop the flood of desire raging through her body.

"Everything." He probed her mouth, his tongue tangling with hers until she moaned and trembled. "You let me into your life," he whispered against her kiss-swollen lips. "And I'm in it to stay."

Her eyes flew open. "Are you saying you're . . ." She swallowed heavily, hesitating to verbalize the wish she'd been repressing for days. ". . . you're in *love* with me?"

"Love is for teenagers." He eased aside the collar of her sweater and pressed his lips to her neck. "I care about you. I want you. I need you. We're good together."

Nila was so stunned by his cool statement, she couldn't find her voice. Bleakly, she realized she had been willing to settle for a loveless but companionable marriage with Frank. Not with Jake, though. Never with Jake. A part of her heart was already his.

His fingers began tracing erotic patterns on her neck. As his lips caressed her temple, she felt the desperation in him and understood that he meant to assert his claim on her.

Why was he doing this? He'd made it clear

he didn't love her. Wanting and needing weren't enough to hold a man like Jake. He was too accustomed to living dangerously. Physical desire was a fickle thing. How long would it take before he grew restless and bored with her? A week? A month?

Desperation began to build inside Nila, a different kind than the one consuming Jake. She knew she had to do something to douse the sexual tension heating between them or they would end up in bed again. Then she would be beyond caring how easily he could break her heart. She wouldn't have the will to resist letting him stay with her.

Jake would leave her sooner or later. *The men in her life always left.*

No! she silently screamed. She refused to set herself up for such emotional pain. Frantically, she pushed at his chest. It was like trying to move a block of granite. "Jake, stop it, please!"

She realized she wasn't getting through to him. "Dammit, I said stop." She grabbed hold of his hair and pulled. "I don't know any of those sneaky little karate tricks like the one you used on Angie."

"Aikido," he murmured before nipping her earlobe.

"What? I don't care what it was. Let me go or I swear I'll pull your hair out by the roots."

It took a moment for her struggles to penetrate the sensual fog engulfing Jake. Distress blended with vulnerability in her brown-gold eyes, reminding him of a frightened doe. He reluctantly released her. "What's wrong, sweetheart?"

"You track me down, turn my life into a three-ring circus, ruin my reputation, and claim I *belong* to you. That's what's wrong."

She surged past him, fists clenched at her sides. "You said yourself you're not in love with me.

Solid, lasting relationships aren't built on great—"
She turned bright pink. "—good sex."

"At least we agree on that point. It was great good sex," he said humorously. He moved toward her, but stopped when she backed away.

"It's a moot point. It's not enough to sustain a relationship. We have nothing in common. I'm a square peg in a small town. You're something straight out of 'Miami Vice'! At best our relationship would be temporary. I don't want a temporary lover."

Jake's heart ached as understanding dawned. She didn't trust him. Being abandoned by a father at an impressionable age, her mother's marriages, and the fickleness of her fiancé were enough to leave scars on any psyche. He wouldn't blame her if she distrusted all men.

He mentally kicked himself. Maybe Rae was right and he was losing his touch. Then again, how could he have known about her deep-rooted fears? He didn't know her well enough. And that was the crux of the problem. They simply hadn't taken the time to learn much about each other.

"You're afraid to trust me," he said softly. "I can understand that. We skipped the getting-acquainted stage and went straight to intimacy. I'm sorry, sweetheart. I thought we would have plenty of time on the island to get to know each other. But you left before we could do that."

He waited for a moment, watching her shift nervously from one foot to the other. "Maybe it did happen too soon, but I do not regret making love with you. My instincts told me that we belong together on some fundamental level. I think you know it too."

"It shouldn't have happened at all. It would be best if we both admit it was a mistake."

He shook his head, wishing he could simply take her in his arms and kiss her resistance away. "We need a chance to get to know each other. Don't be so quick to deny what we could have together simply because you're afraid it won't last."

Mixed emotions clouded her eyes. She looked down at the floor, avoiding his gaze.

He went to her and laid the tips of his fingers on her cheek. She didn't pull away from him. He took that as a positive sign. "I don't want to be without you, Nila. Give me a chance. You may find we have more in common than you think. The only way we'll ever know is if we both give it our best shot. Let me stay with you."

"Jake, I don't know . . ." Nila began, but she realized it was hopeless. She couldn't bear to think of sending him away. She wanted him to stay. But did she have the courage to risk falling deeper in love with him?

"Let me stay, sweetheart." His fingers trembled as he buried his hands in her hair and tipped her head back.

Nila's senses swam as she met his gaze. It was one of those rare moments when he didn't bother to hide his emotions. In his night-dark eyes was a lonely yearning as powerful as her own.

She prayed his feeling for her ran more deeply than he knew. And there was only one way to make that discovery. She had to give him time. "Okay," she said.

The dimple appeared with his shark's smile.

Instantly her common sense struggled to assert itself. "You can stay. But on my terms. No sex."

He frowned, looked ready to argue the absurdity of her stipulation.

"I'm serious, Jake. You try to seduce me and

you're out of here." Brave words. She doubted she had it in her to carry out the threat. But she hoped he believed she would.

He released her and jammed his hands into his pockets. "No problem. Show me the way to a spare bedroom. I promise not to accidentally wander into yours in the middle of the night." He smiled again. "But if you wander into mine, the rules go out the window."

She shook her head. "We've given the neighborhood enough to talk about today. I can't have you here in the house alone with me. You can check into a hotel or stay in the guest cottage out back."

Minutes later, Jake followed Nila outside. He was not a happy man. All his life he had walked a fine line, but it was a line he had drawn. He didn't like it when other people dictated to him where that line should be. If he wanted Nila, though, he had to agree to her terms.

"You may leave your car here," she told him as they walked across a six-car parking area, heading toward a tall privacy hedge. She led him through an opening in the hedge and along a narrow path of fieldstones.

Jake gazed around him at the jungle of trees, shrubs, and flowers, all showing signs of neglect. A giant magnolia stood in one corner of the lot; its branches would block the sky during the spring and summer. Bird feeders were suspended from the limbs of several trees.

"Originally, this was my great-grandparents' honeymoon cottage," Nila explained when the stone path ended at the door of a small house. "They lived here while the main house was under construction. It's been updated through the years."

"Looks like the honeymoon was over a long time ago," Jake said, noting the peeling exterior paint, once white and now weathered to a ghostly gray. Shutters framed the three windows across the front. One of them was barely hanging on by a hinge.

"It doesn't look like much on the outside." She gave him an apologetic smile. "Until recently, I haven't had the money or the time to make repairs and paint. Fortunately, it's structurally sound. It has a new roof."

She unlocked the door and pushed it open. Jake followed her inside to a large room with a high-beamed ceiling and a stone fireplace at one end. The hardwood floor needed refinishing. A ladder was propped against one wall, and drop cloths, paint cans, and equipment were neatly stacked beside it, waiting to be put to good use.

There was no furniture except for a table for two in the compact kitchen at the rear of the room. Open shelves for storage hung above one long counter, with cabinets below it and a sink in the middle. On each end of the counter were empty spaces where a stove and refrigerator once stood.

The bedroom was in the same shape as the living area, only it contained a mahogany four-poster and a dresser.

"It's not the Bahamas Queen Resort," Nila said as he peered at a huge claw-footed tub in the tiled bathroom. "But it's clean, snug, and warm."

Jake had his own notion of snug and warm. They were in the main house with her. Counseling himself to be patient, he turned to her and smiled. "It'll do for now."

She pushed her sleeves up to her elbows and stood looking at him as though she didn't quite know what to say. "I'm sorry the painting isn't done. I had planned to start in the living room this weekend."

"I can do it for you."

"That's not necessary."

He took her hand and felt the chill of her fingers. "It will give me something to do while you're working during the day."

She stepped back, wrenching her hand from his. "Well, you get settled in. I'll bring you linens and towels." Her gaze fastened on his mouth, and he saw her nervously lick her lower lip. He wanted to shake her or kiss her for making things for more difficult than he felt was necessary.

"You'll need a few other things, I guess." She backed up another step. "A coffee pot, soap, a lamp for the—the bedroom." She turned and quickly walked away.

Jake watched her go, wondering how long it would take to win her trust.

Jake's sleep was filled with refracted dreams. He felt the weapon in his hand pressed against the temple of a cold-eyed drug dealer. He smelled fear and recognized it as his own. Then blood-lust shredded the fear. He heard the death knell of a gun being cocked. Sanity screamed a warning inside his head. It faded into the soft, soothing sound of Nila's voice. Her sweet face was close to his as she covered him with her body, holding him. He heard moans and passionate pleas. His or hers?

He woke up shaking, breathing hard. Hair fell into his eyes as he sat up. He was barely aware of combing it back with his fingers.

The nightmare weighed heavily on him, its darkness familiar territory. He took it with him wherever he went. It slept where he slept.

Jake rubbed his face, then glanced at his watch. Two A.M. He got up and left the bedroom.

Instinctively feeling his way through the cottage, he went to the door and opened it. He stood there, looking out into the night.

Moonlight embraced him. Crisp fall air touched his face and he breathed in its clean, fresh smell. Trees swayed as the wind sang a low, sweet song through their almost barren branches.

The wheels of his soul turned, grinding harshly. He had left his job because he feared it would destroy him. His roots were locked into the futility of crusades against greed and crime. He'd done his best and it had nearly taken his soul in return.

He breathed in deeply as though trying to relieve himself of a cumbersome burden. His gaze locked on the roofline of the main house, where Nila slept—untroubled, he hoped, by night demons.

Need for her throbbed painfully in his chest. He needed her beside him, holding him, filling him with her softness and the purity of her spirit. Determination strengthened his resolve not to sleep alone any longer than necessary.

He folded his arms, leaned against the doorjamb, and took comfort in knowing she was near.

Nila lay in bed silently beseeching the sandman to visit her. And she hoped the little devil brought a sledgehammer instead of sand. Maybe then her traitorous body would stop remembering how exquisite it felt to make love with Jake.

She thought of him alone in the guest cottage. He would never fit into her world. A few weeks of boring domestic life with her would send him running to Miami, begging for the excitement of his perilous job.

If only he were a different man, say a respectable lawyer, or a salesman. If only she were a different woman, more adventuresome, a fearless risk taker. But he wasn't, and she wasn't, and it would never work.

It was crazy to allow him into her life. But how could she keep him out of it when he was so determined to stay? Her desire to change his mind about love was even crazier. As she lay there a deep sense of foreboding and a growing feeling of being trapped in a situation out of her control rose within her.

"What have I done?" she whispered to the darkness.

Six

A little past eleven the next morning Nila came home from church to find Jake in her kitchen. He was sitting at the table, drinking her coffee and thumbing through her newspaper as though he had done so a thousand times before.

"Good morning," he mumbled, without looking up.

Nila glared at him. Having spent the night and one church service working herself up to a fury, she was in no mood to be gracious. She mentally added "breaking and entering" to her list of reasons why she shouldn't get involved with Jake Madison.

"Well, I hope you're happy." She threw her purse on the table.

"As a matter of fact, I am." He squinted at her from behind *The Richmond Times*. "I like spending a lazy Sunday morning lingering over coffee and the newspaper. You look cute in that pink thing."

Nila wasn't certain which miffed her more, his cheerful attitude or his calling her worsted wool crepe suit a "pink thing." The suit was as timeless and classic as her long double strand of pearls, ivory silk charmeuse blouse, and ivory heels. Never mind that Angie called it a "Junior Service League disguise." She marched over to the coffee-pot and poured herself a cup.

"I gather I'm not supposed to be happy," he said. "What am I not supposed to be happy about?"

She turned around. Jake had lowered the paper to the table and was now looking at her with his dark unreadable gaze. "Everyone is talking about the *amusing* incident at Books, Gifts & Things yesterday." Flames of embarrassment flared in her cheeks. "Your unfortunate remark about my staying in bed with you in the Bahamas received more lip service than the sermon." Her eyes narrowed. "The sermon was on sins of the flesh."

Jake watched her curiously. "Does it matter so much what they think?"

"Of course! They're my friends, my neighbors, my customers. I don't want them thinking I'm a . . ." She simply couldn't bring herself to say the word she was thinking.

"Come sit down, sweetheart. You've had a rough morning." He pulled out a chair for her.

She dug her heels in and stayed where she was. "There's even a rumor going around about a certain DEA agent coming to town to bust up a drug cartel in Danville." There, that ought to swipe the smile off his face.

It did. He looked pained. "Aw, hell." He ran his hand over the back of his neck in a tired gesture that roused her unwilling sympathy. "How did that idiotic rumor get started?"

"Billy," she said, naming the young policeman who had been so impressed with Jake.

"I told that kid I was retired."

"Apparently he didn't believe you." She sat down

at the table with him. Ridiculous as it was, she decided she must tell him the rest. "Billy has a theory. You see, he's got it in his head that illegal drugs are being brought in by rowboat on the Dan River."

Jake shook his head. "That's a pretty farfetched theory, considering what I've seen of the river."

"It is farfetched. Billy's just seen one Dirty Harry movie too many. I doubt you'd find anything but snakes floating in the Dan River."

He smiled again, and Nila felt little arrows piercing her flesh. Heat swept through her. She didn't think she'd ever felt a smile so physically before.

Attraction sizzled between them. It was so strong, she wouldn't have been surprised if it burst into a swirling ball of fire. His eyes were unmasked, and she knew he felt it too.

She sat back. "I . . ." What? Her mind was a wilderness of jumbled emotions and thoughts.

"What?" he asked softly, startling her by echoing her confused thought.

"I want to know how you got into my house," she said, covering her bemusement with irritation. "I locked the door when I left."

"Trade secret. Your locks are worthless, by the way. Anyone could break in and rob you blind."

Her temper flared. "How arrogant. You're not even sorry about breaking into my house."

"You need a good security system. I'll have one installed for you."

"No you won't. *I* will do it if I want one."

"You're spoiling for a fight," he said evenly. "What's really bothering you? Is it the gossip?"

"Yes. No. A little of both." She sighed. "This isn't going to work, Jake. What are you going to do while you're here? You told me you loved the excitement of your job. I can't imagine you being happy just puttering around. Do you have any plans?"

"The only plan I have at the moment is for us to get to know each other. I may not know what I want to do with the rest of my life, but I am finished living on the razor's edge."

Nila badly wanted to believe him. "What made you decide to retire?"

His gaze shifted away. "A severe case of burn-out. A smart agent knows when it's time to quit."

She knew there had to be more to it than that. He had told her he'd lived for his job to the exclusion of everything else. Jake wouldn't have walked away from it easily. Something had happened. She was sure of it. Something unspeakably ugly.

Her hand tightened around her coffee cup as she tried to swallow the lump of fear in her throat. "I read an article once about undercover narcotics police officers. Some became so disillusioned they couldn't cope with their jobs. Some of them were chemically dependent from being forced to sample the drugs they were supposed to buy. Some of them—" She stopped speaking. The look on his face was stone cold.

"Did I get hooked?" he demanded. "Is that what you want to know? Did the drugs and money suddenly start to look good to me?" His tone was so harsh, she wanted to jump up and run. His blazing eyes told her she'd pushed the wrong button.

"Whatever else I may be, Nila, I'm not stupid or corrupt."

"All right, Jake. I'm sorry for mentioning it."

"Don't be sorry. You needed to ask. It's something I would want to know if I were you."

She looked at her hands. They were trembling

slightly. "I believe you. I only brought it up because I was worried about you. You don't have to say anything else."

"But I do," he said savagely. "We're getting to know each other. *Remember?* I don't want any secrets between us. I don't want you looking at me and wondering."

He reached for her hand and held it between his own. "From day one on the job I went in with an attitude that drugs were for suckers. Every dealer from the lowest form of street life to the biggest power-broker knew I didn't sample the product. But the scum that I *pretended* to be didn't mind making money off suckers who did. It was a convincing act. They bought it. I never had to do drugs to show them I wasn't a narc. I never had to walk away from a deal because of it."

A chill streaked along her spine. What he said made sense. She had no doubt he had been a much-feared man. Only a fool would have attempted to cross him once he got that deadly look in his eyes.

They were silent for the longest time, staring at each other across the table.

He lowered the tension with a smile. "You may as well know, the basic tools I worked with were lies and deception. I was an actor whose audience was a foot from my face. My role was to gain their confidence, to make them believe I was one of them, and win their trust. I led them down the garden path, then slammed the gate shut behind them.

"The trick is to learn to immerse yourself in that role for however long it takes and still be able to walk away alive, clean, healthy, and sane enough to live in the normal world."

He got up and came around the table to stand in

front of her. His hands on her shoulders, he urged her to her feet, so that his body nearly touched hers. "That's why I quit, Nila. I can't do it anymore. I want to live in a world that's clean, healthy, and sane."

She leaned against him. He didn't have to tell her she represented that world to him. She knew it intuitively.

His arms went around her, his chin resting on the top of her head. "I could have stayed with the DEA and supervised field agents. But that kind of job doesn't appeal to me."

She looked up at him. "Yes. You'd go crazy being a desk jockey."

He groaned. "Don't look at me like that."

"Like what?"

"Sweet and soft and sexy."

His mouth met hers, wet, open, demanding. Nila responded automatically. All the sizzling energy and electricity that had flowed between them exploded like fireworks. The heat scorched her as the kiss went on and on . . .

Every shift, every movement of his body against hers, each touch, each stroke created fire that swirled inside her. His kiss was wonderful. Magic. Mystery. The sweetest power on earth, and she savored every overwhelming moment of it. She could almost imagine they were back on the island surrounded by cascading waterfalls and the lush, pulsating beat of Bahamian drums.

Jake lifted his head. "Nila . . ."

She smiled, a slow smile that curled around him like a warm blanket. He groaned as her fingers found and stripped away the rubber band wrapped around his hair. Then he felt her fingers knotting in the loose strands. Her lips stroked across his jaw.

Jake tensed. It would be so easy to renew the physical side of their relationship. A part of him wanted to lay her down on the floor and finish what they had started. But in a rational portion of his mind he knew that afterward the passionate woman in his arms would retreat behind her glasses and prim little suit. She simply wasn't ready to accept completely that part of herself, or him.

His mouth covered hers in one last kiss. "Give me a tour," he said huskily, holding her away from him.

Her passion-filled eyes went blank. "What?"

"I want to see the house, your shop."

Nila nodded, anxiety flooding her as she realized how close she'd come to unleashing the wildness locked inside her. She turned and headed out of the kitchen.

Jake quietly followed her.

A long hallway with a beautiful winding staircase divided the first floor. Her shop was on the left side. On the right was the sitting room they'd been in the day before and a small formal dining area.

At the back of the house she led him into a room with a crystal chandelier, marble fireplace, and gracious furniture from a bygone era. She called it the music room. A gleaming black baby-grand piano covered by a square of lace stood in front of the window. A huge silver candelabra rested upon the piano. One candle was crooked. He smiled, thinking how that one crooked candle kept the room from being too perfect.

It was there that Jake began to understand some of the events that had shaped her life. She drew his gaze to a gilt-framed oil portrait hanging above the fireplace. It showed her mother, Emma, as a young woman in a sparkling tiara and dazzling white gown. He listened to Nila telling him of the beauty contest her mother had won at some festival. Her sister had claimed the same title twenty years later.

They toured the upper floors. He listened carefully as she spoke of childhood memories. Every so often he posed equally careful questions and stored the information in his analytical brain.

Her sister's girlhood bedroom was a shrine of photos and trophies. Nila related several stories of beauty pageant victories and high school triumphs. None of those stories were her own.

He roamed around her bedroom. White lace curtains covered the windows. A white lace counterpane was smoothed over a four-poster bed. The wallpaper was a rosebud print. A part of her was like those rosebuds, he mused, tightly closed, waiting to bloom.

The round tower room fascinated him. He stood at its window, absorbing the treetop view. She told him she had spent many solitary hours there as a child, reading and dreaming.

As Jake followed her back down the stairs the image in his mind was complete. He saw a shy child, a quiet and lonely one, who felt she didn't fit into her family of beautiful extroverts. She identified with her father, a solemn man who hadn't been able to find his place in the scheme of things either. It saddened him to realize she didn't know she was every bit as lovely as her mother and sister, who sounded more self-involved than Nila could ever be.

By the time they entered Books, Gifts & Things, Jake knew it was going to be tough convincing her of her own worth. She was smart, kindhearted, passionate, and beautiful. Somehow he would have to help her see that. It wouldn't be easy. It was obvious to him that she was too used to allowing the judgments and opinions of others to get in the way of her own feelings.

"I like your shop," he said sincerely. "It's warm and friendly. You've made it into a place people feel comfortable in no matter whether they come to buy, browse, or just have a cup of coffee. You've done well, Nila."

She beamed at his praise. Jake made a mental note to give her the positive strokes she so richly deserved.

"It smells delicious in here." He inhaled the enticing aroma of coffee beans. "I don't see how a customer could leave without buying one of these coffees."

She smiled. "Everyone says that. I'm so used to the smell myself that I don't notice it unless I've been away for a while." She turned and moved on into the gourmet foods and gift section of the shop.

An attractive display of old-fashioned toiletries caught Jake's attention. The soaps, bath oils, lotions, and sachets all came in various scents, like almond, rosewater, violets, vanilla, rum, and— He did a double take. "Pine-scented bath oil?"

She laughed at his dubious expression. "You'd be surprised how popular it is." She opened a bottle and held it out to him.

He bent down to sniff the contents, and his nose wrinkled at the heavy scent of pine. "I can't imagine crawling into bed with someone who smells like a forest."

"To tell you the truth, neither can I." She laughed again as she put the bath oil back on the shelf.

"Now this is more my style." He picked up a bottle of apricot body and massage oil. "'Softens the skin,'" he read aloud from the label. "'A silky smooth experience.'" He removed the gold cap and dabbed a bit of oil on his finger, then rubbed his thumb and finger together, coating each with the glistening essence of apricot.

Nila found herself holding her breath as he came toward her with a wicked glint in his eyes. It took all the willpower she possessed to hold still when he drew his finger along her jaw and down her throat. His touch was gentle. The oil was heated to a satiny warmth from his own body heat. In her mind she saw herself naked, and she could swear the same image played in his imagination. His thumb skimmed over the pulse point in her throat, stroking, seducing.

Such wonderful hands, she thought, succumbing to the erotic moment. "Jake," she said, her voice husky and breathless.

"I like this." He lowered his head. His mouth was inches from hers, and she thought he was going to kiss her. Instead he nuzzled her neck with his nose. "Smells nice. How does it feel?" he asked, straightening.

"Warm. Good." So warm and good she felt like melting.

He looked at her with the eyes of a lover, teasing her senses, holding her gaze until she could only see him through a sensual haze.

"Hold out your hand, sweetheart."

She obeyed. He took her hand, then she felt the sleeves of her jacket and blouse glide up her arm. Her eyes closed. A drop of oil was poured onto her wrist. His fingers brushed over her skin, fingers that stroked confidence and pleasure. So sensual. So unerringly sensual. Fire and ice seemed to flow through her veins as sensations surrounded her.

His lips replaced his fingers. Where they touched her, she burned.

"Will you have dinner with me tonight?"

Dinner? Her eyes flew open. Unable to speak, she simply nodded.

He smiled and released her hand. Recapping the bottle, he said, "Start a tab for me, Nila. I'm taking this with me."

Still speechless, she watched him walk away.

At the door, he turned and smiled, lifting the body and massage oil in a salute. "Someday soon," was all he said.

His unspoken promise hung in the air long after he had disappeared from her sight.

Completely unnerved, Nila slumped against the display of toiletries. Dear heavens, she thought dismally. She could no longer deny that she loved that man to distraction. How could she possibly resist him when he could strip away her willpower and good sense with a mere touch?

Half an hour later Jake prowled through the overgrown jungle surrounding the cottage. His encounter with Nila had left him wound up tight. Too tight.

Not far from the cottage he found a grassy spot beside a stone bench. Scooping up an acorn, he put it on the bench. He sat down on the ground a few feet away, in the lotus position, then took a deep breath and concentrated on emptying his mind.

Breath in. Breath out. He focused on the acorn, imagining it as a small brown dot. He stared at the dot until it grew larger, larger, larger. Then he was inside it.

He pictured a crystal ball, pure as a teardrop

diamond on a polished black marble surface. He saw it rising. It floated toward him and hovered just beyond his reach. He held it suspended in midair with the force of his will.

Slowly the crystal ball descended. Jake blinked and came out of his self-induced trance just before the ball touched the ground.

Balanced. Centered. Relaxed. Back to himself, the coiled tension no more a part of him.

Jake rose. He had reached a successful level of concentration. The pouring out of *ki*, his father had called it. Universal cosmic power.

Hands extended, fingertips out. *Ki* to *ki*. Jake began his *kata*, a series of aikido practice forms. Meditation combined with the physical workout had been his salvation for a long time. He moved in small, delicate circles, keeping his balance centered deep within his abdomen.

He had been going through his *kata* for half an hour, when his silent alarm went off in his head. He knew without doubt he was being watched. Keeping his point, he spun in place.

His gaze searched the area until he saw a pair of eyes. Two pairs, actually. They belonged to a child and some kind of animal.

He stared at them. They stared back between the browning leaves of a tall shrub.

Jake's curiosity peaked, yet he remained still and silent. Children were a mystery to him. Having had little contact with the creatures, he simply didn't know how to deal with them. He went with his instinct, which told him a wrong move, a careless word, and this particular little creature might bolt.

There was a twitching movement, then small hands parted the branches. An owlish face appeared. Tufts of fine blond hair stuck up here and there over the child's head as though he'd forgotten to comb it that morning. Thick glasses covered myopic blue eyes.

Jake returned the child's openly assessing gaze, continuing to remain still.

After a long moment, the boy stepped out into the open. Jake knew he was still being sized up. If he didn't pass the inspection, he had a feeling the kid would pop back into the bushes like the mouse in the teapot in *Alice in Wonderland*.

"Hello?" The boy's greeting sounded like a question.

"Hello."

Jake heard more rustling in the shrub. The child turned, reached in, and came out with the fattest, ugliest tiger-striped cat Jake had ever seen. The boy set the animal down on the grass, then they both eyed Jake thoughtfully.

"Who's your friend?" Jake asked.

"My cat, Sugar Booger."

Jake nodded as though it made perfect sense to give a feline such a preposterous name.

"Are you Nila's friend?" the boy asked.

"Yes."

"She's my friend too." The boy approached him slowly.

The cat's gaze followed his master, as though he were trying to decide if accompanying him was worth the energy he would have to exert.

"In fact, Nila is my godmother." The child's tone of voice was absurdly grown-up. He came within arm's length of Jake and stopped. "Are you familiar with spiders?"

"Not really."

The child's eyes flickered as though Jake had just failed an important test. "That's too bad. They are the civil engineers of the world of nature.

Fascinating creatures. Their webs are marvels of geometric design and workmanship."

Jake nodded again. The kid couldn't have been more than what? Five? Six tops. A baby Einstein brain in a tiny Woody Allen body.

He hunkered down next to the boy, getting his eyes on the same level. "Early one morning I went outside. During the night, a spider had spun a giant web across my patio. It was wet with dew drops. The sun made the beads of moisture sparkle like thousands of tiny diamonds. It was quite an impressive sight."

The child's eyes flickered again, this time with approval. "My name is Miles Parker. I believe you met my mother yesterday."

This kid belonged to Angie Parker? He certainly hadn't inherited her looks, beyond the color of his hair and eyes.

"I'm Jake Madison."

"Yes, Mr. Madison, I know. My mother told me about you. I saw you, too, through the window of Nila's bookstore after Aunt Clover called the police."

"Was that before or after they tried to arrest me?" Jake asked, grinning.

"During. Your hands were cuffed behind your back. It must have been an interesting experience. What were you doing a few minutes ago?"

"You may call me Jake. I was practicing aikido."

"Ah, yes. I thought it was some form of martial arts." Miles nodded wisely. "Aikido is a method of hand-to-hand fighting similar to jujitsu. I've read about it in the encyclopedia. It's relatively new compared with other Asian fighting systems. Who taught you?"

"My father. He was an aikido master."

"My father's dead." It was a matter-of-fact statement unaccompanied by so much as a blink.

"So is mine."

The kid's eyes went thoughtful. "If you will teach me aikido, I will teach you about spiders."

"It would be my honor to be your teacher." Jake extended his hand.

"And mine to be yours," Miles solemnly responded, offering his small, soft child's hand in return. They shook on the deal.

Jake rose. "The first thing an aikido student must learn is to fall without injury."

"Are you going to be my friend as well as my teacher?"

"You may count on it. Now observe carefully. Concentration is very important. Try to copy every move I make."

The cat watched them for a moment, then his tail twitched once as though putting a seal of approval on their efforts. Sugar Booger rolled over onto his back and went to sleep.

A short while later, Nila strolled toward the guest cottage. She stopped when she caught sight of Jake and Miles in a small clearing a few yards away. Neither seemed to notice her presence, as they were involved in some sort of graceful exercise. At least, the man's movements were graceful. The boy struggled awkwardly, his limbs so thin and small she feared they would break.

She could see Miles's tiny face pucker with lines of concentration. When he tried valiantly to copy the rolling, leaping technique Jake was showing him, the child tumbled face down on the ground.

Nila pressed her folded hands to her lips to stifle a cry. The child didn't appear to be hurt, though, and she breathed a sigh of relief. Then she heard him laughing!

The child's laughter was gold, doled out rarely in small increments. She knew without a doubt that if Jake hadn't already stolen her heart, she would have given it to him for his ability to make Miles laugh.

He bent over the boy, looking so big and Miles so very small. He picked the child up and set him on his feet.

She was too far away to catch the words Jake spoke to Miles, but she could hear the sound of his voice. His tone was gentle and infinitely patient. Such gentleness and patience from a man who could induce fear with a single glance. Tears of pride welled up in her eyes.

She turned and slipped quietly away.

As she walked back to the house, Nila carried the image of the man and boy she loved in her heart. One of her goals in life was to fill her home with a family of her own. She couldn't help wondering if Jake had ever considered having a family. Probably not, she thought, sighing. Living on the razor's edge didn't seem compatible with the idea of home, hearth, and a desire to hear the patter of little feet.

DON'T HOLD BACK!

1. No obligation! No purchase necessary! Enter our Sweepstakes for a chance to win!
2. FREE! Get your first shipment of 6 Loveswept books *and* a lighted makeup case as a free gift.
3. Save money! Become a member and about once a month you get 6 books for the price of 5! Return any shipment you don't want.
4. Be the first! You'll always receive your Loveswept books before they are available in stores. You'll be the first to thrill to these exciting new stories.

Give in to love and see where passion leads you!
Enter the Winners Classic Sweepstakes and
send for your FREE lighted makeup case and
6 FREE Loveswept books today!

(See details inside.)

Detach here and mail today.

Seven

At seven o'clock Sunday evening Jake stood on the back porch of Nila's house. He tugged at the sleeves of his white shirt and leather jacket. Second thoughts entered his mind about wearing jeans. He brushed those qualms aside. It was ridiculous to feel nervous about what he wore. After all, they weren't going out, which was a sore point with him. He'd intended to take her to a nice restaurant, but she'd come to his cottage late that afternoon and told him she'd prefer eating at home.

His hand was on the doorknob before he reconsidered his intention of letting himself in. She hadn't been too pleased with his uninvited entry that morning. He rapped on the door instead.

Nila answered on his second knock. She was dressed in jeans, too, and a sweater with a cowled neck that covered her from jaw to thighs. Her breasts raised an attractive swell under the soft apricot fabric. The color brought out the fresh, healthy glow of her face. As it had the first time he had seen her, the gold buried in her dark hair and eyes grabbed his attention and held it.

She stared at him appraisingly, a half smile playing about her lips. He stared back. He wanted to reach out and—

"You look beautiful," he said, repressing his desires. "The color of ripe apricots suits you."

A flush of pleasure stained her cheeks. He knew she was remembering the incident with the massage oil and his unspoken promise.

"Thank you. Please come in." She sounded as nervous as he felt. "Dinner is almost ready. I hope you like chicken and pasta."

"I like pasta any way I can get it."

Her smile was disarming. He would eat chocolate-covered ants if she served it to him with a smile like that.

Jake closed the door and followed her into the kitchen. The room was warm, cozy, and filled with appetizing aromas. An ivory linen cloth covered the table. Fresh cut flowers in a glass bowl and candles made an attractive centerpiece. Something classical was playing softly on the radio set on the windowsill above the sink.

She took his jacket from him and hung it on a peg by the door. "Would you mind fixing the salad while I set the table? All the ingredients are on the counter."

He nodded, then inhaled deeply, willing his body to relax as he started to work. What that woman did to him just by being in the same room ought to be a crime.

"Are you comfortable in the cottage?"

"It's fine." He met her gaze for moment.

She clearly understood the look he gave her. It said, "But I'd rather be here with you," and he saw her hand tremble as she lit the candles.

As she arranged plates and silverware on the table, Nila watched Jake. There shouldn't be anything sexy about a man grating a carrot, she told herself, but there was. Maybe it was because it was *Jake* grating the carrot, and everything he did seemed erotic to her.

Love for him spread through her as suddenly as an out-of-control fire. Instant inferno. Lord, it felt good. Good but terribly frightening. Anything so good, anything that mattered so much, would hurt so badly when it didn't last.

She went to the refrigerator and took out a bottle of wine. In her heart she wanted to love and be loved in return. Would Jake be able to return her love? Or would her hopes and dreams go unfulfilled?

In spite of her misgivings, Nila was determined to enjoy his company tonight. As for tomorrow . . . Well, it would come soon enough.

"Are you sure you won't mind painting the cottage?" she asked, placing the chilled chardonnay on the table.

"Not at all. I like working with my hands."

She stared at his hands. Painting would keep those clever hands busy and off certain portions of her anatomy. Somehow that thought didn't make her as happy as it should.

Soon the food was on the table. His praise for her culinary efforts seemed sincere, and she was pleased.

An odd thought occurred to her as she sat across the table from him, and she started laughing.

"What?" he asked.

"We're sharing our first meal together."

"And you find that amusing?"

She nodded. "Our relationship started off so

backwards. Most people have at least shared a meal before hopping into bed."

"I don't think we could have done what we did on full stomachs." He said it with such a straight face that it took her a second to realize he was joking.

She laughed again. "You may be right about that."

Jake fell under the spell of her carefree manner. It was good to see her so relaxed with him. He didn't know why she had lowered her defenses tonight, but he wasn't going to question his luck. It was wise just to appreciate a gift when given one.

"Are you going home for Thanksgiving?" Nila asked, steering the conversation in a safer direction. The traditional holiday was less than two weeks away. Her heart thudded against her ribs as she waited for his reply.

"No. There's no family to go home to. And as for friends . . ." He shrugged. "It isn't easy to maintain real friendships when you disappear for weeks or months at a time."

Compassion stirred in her. "I can't imagine how awful it must be to have no one. My family is far from perfect, but I wouldn't trade them for anything or anyone."

"You also have very loyal friends in the two women I met yesterday."

She briefly closed her eyes in chagrin. "I feel terrible about what happened yesterday. About Angie attacking you. She appointed herself my guardian angel in nursery school and she's been at it ever since. And Clover . . ." She smiled sheepishly. "Well, don't take anything she said personally. Clover's not too high on men in general."

"You have no need to apologize for them. Loyalty is something I've learned to value, because I've seen too many people buy and sell it like a commodity. Rae is the one friend I have whose loyalty is unquestionable."

"Who is Ray?"

"Rae Garcia, my DEA partner. Was my partner," he corrected himself. "She's the closest thing I've got to family. I think you'd like Rae." He smiled fondly. "She's something else."

A green-eyed monster reared up in Nila's chest. She was positive she wouldn't like this Rae person at all. Rae had shared a part of Jake's life that Nila never could. "Is she married?" she asked, keeping her voice light.

"She was years ago." He helped himself to another serving of pasta. "It was over before we started working together. The job was the last nail in the coffin of her marriage. She doesn't talk about it much, but I have a feeling she's still in love with the guy."

Jake stared at the flickering candles for a second, then met her eyes again. "Rae is like me when it comes to caring about people. They're damned few in number, but we'd put our lives on the line for them."

Her eyes widened, and he knew she'd understood the message in his statement. But did she believe it?

"I see," she said in a husky voice that made him wish they were in a different room. That tone of voice belonged in her bedroom with its lacy curtains and—

Jake reined in his wayward thoughts. He doubted it would sit too well with her if he simply picked her up and carried her upstairs. Besides, he'd made his case and now he had to be willing to give her time to think about him and get to know him before she decided if he was trustworthy.

"What happened to your family?" she asked.

"I never knew my mother," he answered matter-of-factly. "I lived in foster homes and then in a children's group home until I was ten. Apparently, my mother was just a kid who couldn't take care of herself, much less an infant."

He met her gaze and saw a strong emotion reflected in her eyes. Her lips were parted as though she wanted to say something comforting but didn't know what. And he could feel the physical connection between them simmering just below the surface.

Nila tried to hide the surge of compassion she felt, for his voice hadn't betrayed any hint that he needed anyone's sympathy. Something he'd said the day before suddenly came back to her. Perhaps he was right about them having more in common than showed on the surface. "What happened when you were ten?"

Another fond smile settled upon his sensuous mouth. "I met Vic Madison when he broke up a street fight I was in."

She almost choked on a mouthful of chicken. "You were in a gang!"

"Not exactly. But I was on my way to being a baaad little dude. I guess Vic saw something worthwhile in me. Thank God."

She silently echoed his sentiment. "Then what happened?"

"Vic was a martial arts expert. He offered to teach me aikido. Since I had been getting the stuffing kicked out of me in that fight"—he grinned—"I decided to take him up on it. I spent every minute I could in the dojo Vic owned. After about six months, I finally got wise and realized Vic wasn't training me to fight. He was training me to be a man, physically, spiritually, morally. He adopted me a year later, and he died when I was in college."

She smiled. "You cared deeply for him."

Jake nodded. "I still miss him." He refilled her wineglass and topped off his own. "Do you expect your mother and sister home for Thanksgiving?"

Her smile went crooked with ruefulness. "Who knows?" she said, waving a hand.

He looked at her questioningly.

"Mama and Mary aren't what you'd call predict-able," she explained. "Mary's in the middle of a messy divorce from her second husband. But I wouldn't be surprised if she breezed in at the last minute. Mama and Tolly may or may not get a wild hair to come home for the traditional gathering at Clover Norville's house."

"Ah yes, your friend with the baseball bat," he said with a teasing grin.

"That's her."

"Who is Tolly?"

Nila pushed her empty plate to one side. "Brad-ley Tolliver, the current love of Mama's life."

"You say that as though the loves of her life have been many."

She nodded, embarrassed that her feelings were so transparent. "Mama likes men. Tall ones. Short ones. Smart or goofy. Bald or hairy. Rich or poor. But all sexy as sin and without a stable, respon-sible bone in their bodies."

Another piece of the puzzle slid into place for Jake. Stable and responsible were the words he picked up on. He had a sinking feeling Nila didn't view him as having either of those qualities him-self. Had her ex-fiancé been endowed with them?

"Actually, I like Tolly," she went on. "He looks like a huggable teddy bear. I think he's been sweet on Mama since they were kids. Unfortunately, poor Tolly is one of the goofy ones." She propped her chin in her hand. "But Tolly isn't as crazy as Mama's third husband. So I have great hopes he'll last for a while."

Jake wondered how many times her mother had been married, but refrained from asking. "Dare I ask what happened to number three?"

"That's what happened to him," she said with a sigh. "He *dared* a train to run over him, and it did."

The wineglass in Jake's hand paused halfway to his mouth. "I beg your pardon? Did you say he was run over by a train?"

She nodded. "In all fairness, we couldn't hold the railroad company responsible. It was midnight and he was dressed in black silk pajamas. The only person who knew about the dare was Mama, and she didn't believe he'd actually go through with it."

Jake stared at her in amazement. Laughter tickled his throat. Inappropriate. Totally inappropriate. "You're kidding. Right?"

"No. I'm not."

Jake could feel himself starting to grin.

"The man was a double order of fruitcake," she said, her eyes sparkling with suppressed laughter. "There was hardly enough left of him to scrape together for the funeral."

Jake cracked up.

She threw her linen napkin at him, but she was laughing too.

"We're horrible—" She hiccupped a giggle. "—awful people—" another hiccupped giggle "—to laugh about something so tragic."

Jake laughed harder. "I can't wait to meet your mother. Is your sister as flaky as she is?"

"I'm afraid so. The last time Mary phoned, she was talking about hiring a hit man to do away with her husband. They were battling over who gets custody of their dog. But she—Mary, not the dog—was in bed with her analyst at the time and I heard him tell her that wasn't a healthy attitude."

Jake shook his head. "How did you manage to grow up so sane?"

She rose and started stacking dishes. "Somebody in the family had to have both feet planted on solid ground."

Another piece of the puzzle. Jake got up to help her. "I'll rinse. You load the dishwasher."

The cleaning up didn't take long. As they worked, Jake considered several ways to frame the question that had been in his mind since Nila had insisted on their not dining out. By the time he handed her the last dish, he decided just to come out with it. "This morning you were upset by what people were saying about us at church. Is that why you refused to go out with me tonight?"

"Jake!" As she turned to look at him, Nila caught a glimpse of a fleeting emotion in his expression. Then his jaw was set in a hard line.

She recognized what that emotion was, though. She had hurt his feelings. It had never occurred to her that she could do that. How stupid. Just because he rarely allowed his emotions to show didn't mean he didn't feel hurt, anger, joy, and sorrow like any human being.

Distress filled her eyes. "Do you think I asked you here because I didn't want to be seen in public with you?"

He nodded. The barrier was still up.

"Well, of course you would think that from the way I behaved and the things I said." She laid her hand on his arm. "Jake, I wanted you here in my home not because I'm ashamed to be seen with you, but because I thought we needed privacy. And I wanted to cook for you."

"Thank you, Nila." The barrier was lowered. Just a fraction. Just enough for her to see a flicker of genuine relief. "That's all I needed to hear."

She felt his hands on her waist. "I told you once I'm not very brave." She kept her gaze locked steadily with his. "The gossip did bother me. I can't guarantee I won't be upset by it in the future. But I agreed to let you stay here with me. It is not my intention now or ever to keep you hidden like a guilty secret." The only guilty secret she hoped to hide was that she was in love with him.

He smiled beguilingly, making her extremely conscious again of the attraction his dimple held for her. "And you claim you aren't brave. You have more courage than you give yourself credit for, sweetheart."

"I saw you with Miles this afternoon."

"Did you now."

She could feel the heat of his gaze caressing her mouth. The tips of her breasts hardened in response. "Uh, I— Were you showing Miles that aikido thing?"

He smiled and drew her into the cradle of his hips. "That's right."

"He's got a genius IQ. Tests right off the charts. He's so smart, sometimes it's scary."

"I could tell." He pressed a light kiss upon her temple.

Nila felt herself weakening, pressed as she was against the long, hard, aroused length of his body. "What else did you notice about him?"

"Who?"

"Miles." She couldn't resist winding her arms around his neck.

"He has a fat, lazy cat."

She kissed his chin. "Be serious."

He tilted his head back to stare down into her eyes. "I've never been more serious in my life. May I sleep with you tonight?"

The passionate woman stirred inside her, and Nila wanted to melt into him. She also wanted to punch his lights out for making her want him so badly. "No."

"Okay."

She breathed a sigh of relief.

A moment later, he said, "Miles has a socialization problem. Right?"

She rewarded him with a warm smile, and he groaned.

"If you keep smiling like that and wiggling against me, I cannot be held accountable for my actions."

"You will always be accountable for your actions," she said, only half in jest.

"Somehow I knew you'd feel that way."

"Miles likes you." Her voice was suddenly serious. "For all his intelligence, he's still just a six-year-old boy. His soul is fragile. He can be hurt so easily. Please, Jake, don't start anything you don't intend to stay around long enough to finish."

Jake was quiet for a moment. She wasn't just talking about the boy, and they both knew it. He supposed it shouldn't have surprised him to learn his motives were still under suspicion. But it did. And it hurt. "I understand what you're saying," he said quietly. "I never make promises I do not intend to keep."

Her brown-gold eyes searched his face. Looking for truth, he supposed. A smile suddenly blossomed on her face, and she twisted out of his grasp. He watched her open a drawer and fish around inside it.

Coming back to him, she said, "Hold out your hand."

He looked down at the key she placed on his palm.

"It's yours. Don't lose it. It unlocks both the front and back doors."

He smiled as his fingers closed over the tiny piece of trust she'd just given him.

On Monday morning the bell above the door of Books, Gifts & Things never seemed to stop ringing. Friends, neighbors, new and longtime customers came in to get the scoop on Saturday's excitement. Everyone was curious about Jake Madison, and all morning Nila fielded questions.

Jake was a new friend she met on vacation.

Yes, a good friend.

No, he was staying in the guest cottage.

No, she didn't know how long he intended to stay.

Yes, apparently he had lived a very exciting life.

And she cleared up a few misconceptions.

He wasn't with the DEA any longer. He was retired.

Jake was visiting her, not investigating a notorious drug ring operating in Danville.

The curious crowd thinned out by noon, until only Angie and Clover remained. Usually, Nila and Angie alternated lunch hours, and several times a week Clover would show up to eat with one of them or just keep them both company.

That day, Nila opted to do something she rarely did. She closed the shop for lunch. Leaving her friends in the kitchen preparing soup and sandwiches, she went out to invite Jake to join them.

Since he seemed determined to get to know her, she figured, he might as well get to know her friends, because they were an important part of her life. Nila grinned. Clover alone was a baptism by fire. If her sharp tongue didn't send him racing back to Miami, then Jake's intentions might very well be serious!

She glanced at his car as she crossed the parking area. The '66 Mustang looked sporty and lovingly preserved, but she had a difficult time seeing it as the kind of automobile he would own. She pictured him in something more sleek and powerful, something that reflected its owner's strength and mastery. Maybe a Porsche in glossy black to match his hair and to hint at the dangerous core inside him.

She strolled along the path, taking her time, stretching out the walk as long as possible. It felt good to be outside in the sunshine, breathing in the crisp scent of fall.

A puff of wind swirled leaves around her. She thought of the countless times during her childhood that she, Mary, and Angie had raked leaves into huge piles, then gleefully dived into them. Had Jake ever known that childish joy? she wondered. Probably not. The city streets of Miami had been his playground.

The front door was standing open when she reached the cottage. She stood on the threshold and peered inside.

Dressed in nothing but faded, age-softened jeans, Jake faced the wall to her right. The denim snugly outlined his flat, masculine buttocks as he bent over from the waist to dip a wide brush into a tray of creamy white paint. He straightened and raised his arm. Using only a controlled wrist motion, he stroked color onto the wall, starting above his head. The brush drifted slowly down. Legs spread apart, he flexed his knees, following the downward movement of his wrist.

Her cheeks grew hot and her palms started to sweat as she watched him. He seemed to be deep into the physical movement, as though the paintbrush were an extension of his exquisite body. He also seemed to be deep into the soft, faintly oriental music filling the room. Desire curled inside her as crazy thoughts whipped through her head.

Jake knew Nila was there. He'd been acutely aware of her since her arrival. Her eyes were upon him. He could feel the heat of her gaze burning into his back.

He waited for her to speak. The brush slowly caressed the wall. Down. Down. He flowed with the movement, flowed with the gentle musical freedom embodied in Kitara's New Age jazz.

"Hello, sweetheart," he said, when she continued to remain silent. "Have you come to inspect my work?"

He turned slowly. They looked at each other as they had once before, when there had been a casino gambling area between them. Sizzling attraction. Instant, primitive recognition. The call of kindred spirits. For a long moment, they were aware of only the music, the wind's whisper, the beating of two hearts, and the shivering need to touch, to make connection.

She slid her palms along her flannel skirt, along her thighs. Her nervous gesture introduced more complications and undercurrents into the river of emotions surging between them.

"No," she said at last. "But you're doing a wonderful job."

There was something fragile in the look she gave him just before she lowered her eyes, and he wondered what had caused it. Was it her uncertainties about him? Or was it simply the results of a rough morning at her shop? Whatever it was, it made him want to draw her into the protective shield of his arms.

This woman belonged to him, he thought. He would do anything to keep her safe and happy.

She met his gaze briefly, then glanced around the room. "You've finished the ceiling. You must have started early this morning."

"Yes. I couldn't sleep."

She smiled. "It looks nice, and I don't see a drop of paint on you. I usually slop as much paint on myself as I do on the walls."

"It's my technique." He flashed her a smile. "Come, I'll show you."

"What is that music?" she asked. Her long skirt swirled around her ankles as she walked toward him.

"Kitara's *Silk Road*." Such a sweet picture she made in her prim clothing, he thought. Today, she hid her passionate nature beneath a plaid skirt of navy, yellow and white, a pleated white blouse, a butter-colored cardigan, opaque tights, and sensible shoes.

"It's beautiful music." She stopped beside him. "Sounds like a mountain stream. I can almost see the sparkling clear water rushing over the rocks."

He smiled his approval, then dipped the brush into the tray and gave it to her. She allowed him to position her in front of him with her body pressed close to his.

"Hold the brush like this." He positioned her fingers and thumb on the handle and curved his hand loosely around her wrist. "Keep your back very straight," he said, running his other hand down her spine until it came to rest upon the swell of her hip.

Fine strands of her hair tickled his cheek, and he couldn't resist kissing her temple. The simple gesture created a shudder of pleasure within him, and he felt that shudder echo through her.

"Close your eyes," he said softly. He turned his head slightly, bringing his mouth into intimate contact with her ear. "Relax. Listen to the music and let it fill up inside you. Imagine the brush is a part of your hand. It's as much a part of you as your skin." He nudged her legs apart with one of his. "Stand with your feet apart like so. Imagine your balance is centered deep in your abdomen."

He closed his eyes as he lifted her arm high above her head. For a moment, he kept still, basking in the pleasure of holding her, of drinking in the scent of her exotic island perfume.

"Jake?" The pleasing, throaty, altogether sexy tone of her voice—the whisper of a fallen angel—reached through the sensual haze engulfing him. "Aren't you going to show me your technique?"

"Yes, sweetheart." He was hard-pressed not to laugh. "I certainly am." He opened his eyes. "Keep your arm extended and move your wrist, only your wrist. Stroke the surface with the brush like this. Keep your back straight. Bend your knees slightly as you draw the brush down."

His knees caressed the back of hers as they followed the downward brush stroke with their bodies. "Balance and harmony. You are balance and harmony in motion." He tilted her wrist up in a graceful movement.

Nila remained silent. She was vibrantly aware of her heightened senses and shocked by her own reckless desire. The music was an aphrodisiac drifting around them, through them, filling them. She felt the hard, muscled tension in his body, felt his heat reaching out to envelop her. An unfathomable pool of emotion and need blotted out everything as she accepted his guidance in a private, sensual dance.

"Nila." He spoke her name in a shattered exclamation that seemed half anguished need and half plea, and she wondered at the desperation she thought she heard too. She shook her head slightly, finding it difficult to imagine this strong, controlled man being desperate about anything.

Confusion and a belated caution were mingling with her own growing desire. Passion always ignited so quickly between them. Much too quickly. She began to doubt the wisdom of remaining so close to him.

"Sweetheart, I'm doing my best to give you time," he said, startling her into thinking he could read her emotions far too well. She could feel him controlling himself with an intense willpower.

"I know you don't understand yet," he went on, "but I *need* you. I need you in ways I can't even explain." He lowered his head to press his mouth against her neck.

Nila felt oddly captivated by his demanding need, and enthralled by her own response. This was the man she loved, the man with whom she could explore the boundaries of her own sexuality. Her eyes closed as her senses were filled with wonder and excitement and the light-headed thrill of it all. The waterfall of sensation overpowered her, leaving her feeling dazed and somewhat frantic.

Aroused beyond belief, Jake could feel his heart pounding against his ribs. His breathing became labored. He burrowed his face in her curtain of hair and whispered her name again.

Unadulterated male possessiveness swam through him. He wanted her so badly. Her own hunger and passion vibrated through her body, and he was certain he could tap into her need and renew his claim upon her. But he was also certain he would be stealing something she wasn't yet ready to give.

Tenderness, protectiveness, and other emotions surged within him. He did not recognize some of those heady emotions, and he did not feel ready to explore them, so he fought to control them. The lesson was getting out of hand. With torturous slowness he let go of her wrist. Stepping back, he cleared his throat. "Well, what do you think of my technique?"

She turned. Her eyes were blazing with arousal and confusion. Then an angry flush rose to her cheeks. "Don't be obnoxious." She slapped the brush into his hand. "You know damn well what I think. Your technique almost set my hair on fire. It's erotic, seductive, and—and—totally uncalled for."

"But fun," he said, grinning. "Lots and lots of fun. You can't deny you were as turned on as I was."

Her flush deepened. "Your arrogance is showing. What kind of game are you playing with me, Jake?"

That stung. Irritation, need, aggression, and passion shot through him. He stood very still for a moment, willing himself to stay calm and cool.

The brush fell to the drop cloth as he stepped forward and caught her face between his hands. An instant later his mouth was covering hers in a kiss that shocked them both.

"This is no game," he said roughly as he lifted his head to stare down at her.

She jerked free. He could see she was nervous, even a little scared, but her eyes still met his with steady determination. "Lunch is ready. I expect you to put on shoes and a shirt. Clover and Angie are eating with us, so plan on behaving yourself, Jake Madison."

He watched her storm away. In spite of his irritation at her refusal to acknowledge the bond between them, in spite of his painful raw emotions, he admired her exit. She couldn't have timed it better to coincide with Kitara's breathtaking musical crescendo, which imitated the exciting elements of a storm. The sound of wind, rain, and thunder filled the room.

His sweet little Nila had claws. Jake grinned. He wouldn't mind getting scratched occasionally.

Nila walked back to the house feeling far more shaken than she wanted to admit. She could still taste Jake's mouth, could still feel his heated passion. Once again he had touched her in ways that could not be dismissed as simply physical. And she had responded instantly, completely.

Frustration and rage rushed through her veins. She had desperately wanted to tell him she loved him. But he didn't want her love. He didn't believe in it. *Love is for teenagers,* he had said.

The realization that she wouldn't be able to keep her secret from him for very long was enough to ruin the rest of her day.

Eight

Jake stopped painting at noon on Wednesday. The rhythm his life had taken on over the past few days was a pleasing one. He was enjoying transforming the drab, neglected cottage into a welcoming, cheerful place, and he was surprised at how much more he was enjoying teaching Miles Parker the art of aikido.

Children were interesting little creatures, he decided as he cleaned up. He was especially fascinated with Miles. The boy's quick, computerlike mind soaked up information faster than Jake could feed it to him. Miles wasn't quite as starved for attention and affection as Jake had been at his age. Still, the boy was in need of male companionship and friendship, and Jake was glad he gave Miles both.

He pulled a black and white sweater over his head, then fished a pair of running shoes out from under the bed and put them on. After brushing his hair and tying it back, he left the cottage to join Nila for lunch.

As he strolled toward the main house, he savored

the rich pleasure he took in the stability and order in Nila's life. He was amazed to find his appreciation for structure and familiarity ran deeper than he had ever imagined. Thanks to her, he felt as though he had stepped out of the chaos of the world and into a lasting peace and quiet.

Only three things marred his contentment: the nightmare, the slow progression of his relationship with Nila, and his uncertainty over his future. He didn't regret that his old life was gone, nor did he like the lost feeling that enveloped him whenever he wondered what he was going to do with himself.

Patience, he thought, as he walked up the steps to the back door. In time, all those questions would be answered.

He found Angie and Clover in the kitchen. Once again lunch was to be a communal affair, but he didn't mind. The two women were tightly woven into the fabric of Nila's life, and he welcomed each opportunity to add himself to the pattern.

He smiled and greeted them. "Where's Nila?"

"She's minding the store," Clover said. "She *works* for a living, unlike some people I could mention."

Jake grinned and ignored her barb. He knew it irritated the daylights out of her when she couldn't get a rise out of him, but it also earned him a certain amount of her grudging respect.

"Jeez, Clover, that's an ugly hat." He came up behind her and tugged on the long feathers that curled down her back. "What kind of bird is that nesting on top of your head?"

"It's a loony bird," Angie called out gleefully as she opened the oven and hauled out a foil-wrapped loaf of bread.

"Oh, funny ha-ha," Clover said. "Go ahead and

laugh at an old lady." She waved a wooden spoon threateningly at Jake. "I know I'm wearing the silliest hat in all creation, but it has sentimental value. It's my—"

"Dead sister's hat," Jake and Angie chorused in dulcet tones.

Clover made a face at them. She stuck the wooden spoon into an enormous pot of home-made vegetable soup that was heating on top of the stove. "Go ahead and make fun," she said as she stirred vigorously. "It don't make no never-mind to me. I'm an old woman and I can wear ugly hats if I want to. Wash your hands, Jake."

He saluted her and did as he was told.

When he went to help Angie set the table, she kissed him on the cheek. "Have I told you I adore you for what you're doing for my son?"

"Twice yesterday, three times the day before that, but not today."

She laughed. "I'm eternally grateful," she said three times. "You've become a role model for Miles. He talks about you constantly."

"Don't make too much of it," Jake said, feeling a strange mixture of pleasure and embarrassment. He'd played many roles in his life, but never had he been anyone's role model. "I enjoy working with Miles. He's a neat kid."

Angie beamed another smile at him. "You're a gorgeous hunk of man, Jake. If Nila didn't have dibs on you, I'd be all over you like cheap uphol-stery on a chair."

"Promises, promises," he said, taking her out-rageous flirting in the spirit in which it was intended. "All I get from beautiful women are promises."

Over the past few days he had learned a great deal about Angie Parker. If he were able to see a person's aura, he would bet hers was a red-hot ring with a sad blue center. She acted more wise to the ways of the world than she really was, and yet was smarter than she seemed too. She was also a tiger where her son and her friends were concerned. Flirting with any available man was simply a part of her style, like the crazy, provocative clothes she wore.

He inspected the attention-getting clothes she had on now. "Angie, that outfit is definitely *you*."

Her *outfit du jour* consisted of black leather high-top shoes, white tights, black bicycle pants that came to her knees, a gauzy white cheerleader-length skirt, and a black silky top covered by a hot pink bolero jacket. Two earrings dangled from one ear. A jaunty hot pink beret was perched on her glossy blond-white hair.

"But of course." She smiled flippantly. "Am I clever or what? As soon as I saw these darling little things I said to myself, Angie—I call myself Angie—"

"I call you a *nut*," Clover said.

"—I said, Angie, this is you babes, too cha-cha for words."

Clover set a soup tureen on the table. "If you dyed your hair purple, you'd look like a punk rocker."

"That's a wonderful idea, Auntie dear." She aimed a kiss at the older woman's cheek. "I do so love being on the cutting edge of fashion."

"Go ahead. Dye your whole head purple. It'll give me a good excuse to cut you out of my will." Clover stomped over to the refrigerator and took out a pitcher of iced tea. "I've always suspected your mother brought the wrong baby home from the hospital. You can't be a member of my family. You're too twisted."

"Who's too twisted?" Nila asked, coming into the kitchen in time to catch that last remark.

"Clover says I am." Angie flashed her trademark smile at Jake. "Do you think I'm twisted, Jake?"

He nodded and said solemnly, "Like a cyclone."

Angie laughed and mock punched his arm.

Nila maintained a pleasant expression as she watched the two people she loved engage in flirty banter. In her head, she knew Angie didn't mean anything by it. It was just a habit her friend had developed to disguise her heartache over the loss of her beloved husband, a wonderfully brilliant man who had been twenty years Angie's senior. Jake didn't appear to take Angie seriously either, but Nila couldn't help being a little jealous of how quickly they had developed an easy friendship.

"How's the painting going?" she asked Jake as they all sat down at the table.

"Great. I finished the bedroom walls. All that's left is the trim work." He ladled the thick vegetable soup into his bowl.

"It's about time something was done about that cottage." Clover passed the loaf of crusty French bread to him. "It's been an eyesore ever since the good Lord was a teenager."

During the meal Nila let the conversation flow around her, noting that Jake was more talkative than a talk-show host. It was another side of him that showed when the four of them were together. He could settle with surprising ease into the role of polished raconteur when he wanted to. Was this the real Jake? she wondered. Or was it just one of the many roles he played so well?

An eruption of laughter startled her, and she realized she'd tuned out for a minute. She looked around to see Angie hanging onto every word Jake said. Clover was laughing so hard, tears were running down her cheeks.

"I'm serious," Jake said. "Things like that happened to me all the time. Like the time my partner, Rae, and I had stopped at a deli to get a sandwich. I'd just bitten into a huge meatball sub when we heard screaming and yelling and running feet outside.

"I go out, with my mouth full of meatballs, just in time to see this woman with a hammer chasing a man. A police car roars down the street with its dome light spinning, but the woman ducks into a doorway and the squad car goes right by her. Next thing I know she's running straight toward Rae and me.

"I'm screaming at her to stop, spraying meatballs and bread all over the place, but she keeps on coming with the hammer raised like she's going to give me forty whacks.

"I scream, 'Stop or I'll shoot!' and raise my hand, praying I won't have to shoot. But there's no gun in my hand. I'm threatening this lunatic with a loaded meatball sandwich!"

Clover and Angie shook with laughter.

"Jake, you're a real piece of work," Clover said, patting her hands to her cheeks. "I can't remember the last time I laughed so hard."

Still chuckling, Angie got up. "It's been fun, but I've got to get back to work." She waggled her hot pink fingernails at them and headed toward the shop.

Jake turned his head to glance at Nila, who was sitting beside him. He told his stories to entertain, to make her laugh, because he loved that warm, melodious sound. But he hadn't heard her laughing. She'd hardly even smiled over the meatball story.

"You're very quiet today, sweetheart. Is something wrong?" he asked, searching her face for clues to what she might be thinking or feeling.

"No, nothing is wrong." Her hands gestured with her words, a graceful flutter underlined by nerves. She lifted one hand to her hair to push it back from her face. Jake noticed a shaft of sunlight from the window streaming over her brown-gold tresses.

"I was just thinking about—" Her gaze darted from his face and bounced around the room, as though she were either trying to recall what she had been thinking or was stalling until she could come up with something. "About the children's books I'm planning to order."

"Well, I hope you're not planning to order any more of those trashy books you've been selling to children," Clover said as she refilled her empty glass with tea.

Nila frowned. "What trashy books?"

Clover rattled off a list of titles.

"But those novels are so popular with the kids, I can hardly keep them on the shelves," Nila said. "The kids love them because they're fun and entertaining."

"It's the same kind of trash they watch on TV. You ought to be stocking good literature," Clover said adamantly.

Nila looked concerned. "Well, I agree those books aren't classics. But don't you think the important thing is that the kids *are* reading?"

"Those books are junk food for the mind," Clover said, tapping her forehead with one finger.

Jake watched Nila chew on her bottom lip. He could see she didn't really agree with Clover, but she was wavering on her own feeling that there wasn't anything wrong with the popular literature the kids loved to read.

"Well, maybe you have a point, Clover," she said at last. "I'll give it some consideration."

Clover nodded in satisfaction. "I'm sure you'll do the right thing. You've always been a very sensible girl." Her hawk eyes strayed to Jake as she stood up. "Well, almost always," she added pointedly.

Jake didn't like the worried expression on Nila's face. Where was the backbone she'd shown him two days ago? Once again he became concerned about her tendency to allow the opinions of others to weigh as much or more than her own. If she let other people overrule her own judgment in a business matter, she might allow their opinions to color her feelings about him.

"I got a letter from your mama," Clover went on as she carried her dishes to the sink. "She enclosed a picture of her and that fool, Tolly, riding mules down the Grand Canyon."

"That's nice," Nila said absently. She got up and started clearing the table. "Don't bother with the dishes, Clover. I'll clean up."

Jake pushed back his chair and helped her.

"Emma said they might fly home for Thanksgiving." Clover turned to Jake. "I always have a big Thanksgiving dinner at my house. If you're planning to stick around, you may come too."

His gaze flickered to Nila. She looked distracted, and there was a line between her brows—frustration, worry, or annoyance? He wanted to go to her and smooth it away. Instead, he turned and stared directly into Clover's eyes.

"I plan to be around for a long time. I would be delighted to have Thanksgiving dinner with you. Thank you for the invitation."

He watched Clover examine his face. After a

moment, she nodded as though satisfied with whatever she had seen. "We'll see." She gave his arm a pat as she headed out of the kitchen. Before she cleared the room, she called out, "Get yourself a haircut, Jake. You look like a girl, for heaven's sake."

He lifted a brow at her parting shot. Glancing at Nila, he saw she was still lost in her own thoughts as she put away the leftovers from lunch.

Silently, he began rinsing dishes and placing them in the dishwasher. What price would Nila pay for the approval of others? he wondered. If he wasn't respectable enough, if he was too different to be accepted by her friends and neighbors, was he then fighting a losing battle trying to be a part of her life?

"Do you think I look like a girl?" he asked, deciding to put his concerns to the test.

"A girl?" she repeated, looking at him in confusion.

"Clover thinks my hair makes me look like a girl," he said. "I want to know what you think."

Nila flushed, remembering how his hair had felt so silky on her skin when they had made love. He could grow his hair down to his toes and perm it, and he would still look like the most virile man on earth to her.

His eyes narrowed into slits of black fury. "Get me a pair of scissors."

"Jake, I—"

"Scissors."

She stared at the hard look on his face. Her failure to answer his question immediately had not only angered him, but had hurt him as well. She hadn't meant to do that.

The silence stretched between them. It apparently stretched beyond his patience. He began opening drawers and searching until he found what he was looking for. "Cut it," he said, coming back to her, scissors in hand. "If I don't look man enough, respectable enough for you, cut it."

She grabbed the scissors and threw them in the sink. "Dammit, Jake, this has gone far enough. I like the way you look. I *love*—" She pressed her lips together to keep from saying she loved him.

Her gaze dropped. "I think you know you're more man than I can handle, and I haven't questioned your respectability since I found out you weren't a professional gambler."

A second later, she found herself backed against the counter with his mouth on hers. She could taste the residue of his anger, but she also tasted his need, and she surrendered to it. Her arms went around him. Her body strained against his. Wanting became a mindless whirl of desire only he could ignite inside her.

Nila felt totally possessed by him. In long strokes his hands ran from her shoulders to her wrists and back again. Her mouth burned from the urgency of the hard, hot kiss. All she could want was more.

When he lifted his head, she sagged against the counter, watching him while she struggled to catch her breath, while she waited for her heart to stop trying to pound its way out of her chest, while she fought to break through the torrent of physical and emotional sensations.

"Sweetheart." He raised one hand to her face. "What are you going to do about me?"

"I don't know," she whispered. Tears stung the back of her throat and eyes. "I've thought about it constantly, and I can't find an answer. You make me feel different than I've ever felt before. It's scary, Jake."

His hand slid down to his side. "Yes, I imagine it is."

She struggled to ask calmly, "What do you really want from me?"

"The same thing I want to give you. Everything two people want and need in each other. Loyalty. Commitment. A lifetime of both. I think we should get married."

Panic competed with a flood of pleasure. She looked up at him through wet, spiky lashes. "You don't mean that."

"Yes, I do. You triggered something in me right from the start. I may not know what I want to do with the rest of my life, but I do know I want to live it with you."

Her panic escalated. He wanted to marry her. *But he didn't love her!*

"You don't have to give me an answer now." He smiled ruefully. "In fact, I wish you wouldn't, because I know what it would be. All I ask is that you listen to your instincts. Trust your own judgment about me, about my hair, about the kind of children's books you order."

He gave her a quick, sweet kiss.

Thoroughly confused, Nila called his name as he headed for the door. He turned to look at her. "What does your hair and my children's book order have to do with one another?"

"Think about it, sweetheart. Whose opinion is more important to you? Someone else's or your own?"

She stared at him wide-eyed until the door closed behind him. He could read her far too well. He'd picked up on one of her insecurities. How long would it be before he guessed how deep her feelings for him actually were?

Maybe he already knew. Maybe that was why he'd told her he wanted to marry her.

She forced away the barrage of emotions swimming through her.

If only he loved her, she thought sadly as she headed back to the shop.

"Jake was a riot at lunch today," Angie said, artfully arranging goodies in a gift basket a new father had ordered for his wife upon the birth of their first child. "I could listen to his stories all day long. I can just see him waving a meatball sandwich at that crazy woman." Her silvery laugh filled the shop.

"He's lucky he didn't get his head bashed in," Nila said, putting the finishing touch to the huge pink bow she was making.

"He's wonderful. I'm so happy for you." Angie wrapped colorful cellophane paper around the basket, then picked up an instrument resembling a hair dryer and turned it on. "Jake's in love with you, and I'm eaten up with envy," she said, moving the instrument lightly over the basket to make the cellophane shrink around it.

"I wish that were true." Nila sighed heavily.

Angie switched off the dryer and set it down. "Of course it's true. You love him, don't you?"

"Yes." Nila tied the pink bow on the topknot of cellophane, avoiding her friend's concerned gaze.

"Then what's the problem?"

"Oh, Angie, it's so complicated. I fell for Jake the night we met. It scared me to death then and it scares me even more now." She glanced up. "He doesn't believe in love!"

"Doesn't believe in love?" The bemused, troubled expression on Angie's face mirrored Nila's feelings. "I don't understand. I could swear he loves you. It's so obvious whenever he looks at you."

Nila poured out the entire story of how they'd met and what had happened between them, concluding with Jake's proposal of marriage. "So you see, it's all so mixed up. I've come to know him well enough to trust him. I don't doubt he cares for me and needs me. But he can't give me his love. And that's what I want from him."

A tear slid down her face. She angrily brushed it away with the back of her hand. "He only has to touch me to make me want him. It frightens me to know anyone can have such complete power over my will.

"I was willing to settle for a marriage without love with Frank. But I can't with Jake. I just can't. And I can't make him feel something he doesn't." She hugged her arms to her chest and leaned back against the work counter. "I don't even know what he sees in me, and I'm afraid to even let him know I love him."

"Maybe he's afraid to love you. Ever think about that?" Angie asked, dropping down on a stool in the small work space.

"Impossible," Nila said. "Jake doesn't know the meaning of fear."

"Not impossible." Angie picked up her cigarette case and lighter. "We human beings are perverse creatures. We want intimacy and love, but it scares us." She smiled wryly and lit a cigarette.

"It doesn't scare Jake, and it doesn't scare you. I wish I could be more like you. You never have problems with men."

"I'm not exempt from having problems with men," Angie said coolly. "I'm just as scared as you are where men are concerned." She exhaled smoke along with a sigh. "I've known the most all-consuming love, and it was taken away from me."

Compassion filled Nila's heart. "I'm sorry, Angie. You still miss Jon, don't you?"

"Not a day goes by that I don't miss him. I know people thought I was crazy for marrying him. He wasn't handsome or rich. Jon was shy, gentle, sweet, and thoughtful. I *adored* him because he saw through my flamboyant ways to the person I am inside. He loved me in spite of all my faults. In my eyes, he was perfect. The love we shared was so special." She paused to stub out her cigarette. "I'm afraid I'll never know that kind of love again."

Angie blinked back tears as she reached for Nila's hands. "I feel like we're sisters. I want the best for you. I want you to have the kind of love I shared with Jon. If that's how you feel about Jake, fight for your happiness. Don't let your insecurities rule your heart."

They held each other's hands tightly, feeling closer than ever in the face of their sorrows and fears.

The rest of the week slipped by. Jake made no further mention of marriage. He reined in his feelings in an effort to allow Nila the space and freedom she needed to come to terms with her feelings and with him.

Every day he worked on the cottage until Miles arrived for his aikido lesson after school. He had come to treasure the boy's rare smiles and the sound of his laughter. And Jake decided that maybe it wasn't necessary for him to try to save the whole world in order to enjoy inner peace. The small effort of teaching Miles aikido, of passing along Vic's philosophies, of helping the boy to feel good about himself, created the same serenity.

Every day and night he spent as much time with Nila as she would allow. They had coffee together each morning before she opened the shop and lunch together each afternoon. Wednesday night he took her out to dinner and to see a movie at the local theater. The next evening, after she closed the shop, they sat in the gazebo at the end of the veranda and watched the sun set. Neither of them spoke as the sun performed its miracle in the sky. Jake counted that moment as one of the best in his life.

Friday night, he talked her into letting him give her an aikido lesson. When he showed her a series of slow, graceful movements, she seemed as fascinated as Miles was. She listened carefully to his explanation of the mystical concept of *ki*, but was obviously skeptical of the notion that a universal cosmic power provided mental, physical, and spiritual control.

He went on to tell her that the balance necessary to aikido was the same as the balance necessary for everything in life. "For too long my life had no balance," he said. "Now I'm finding it again with you."

The lesson ended when she kissed him so sweetly, his heart twisted in his chest.

Jake would have been content to idle on as they were if it weren't for the nightmare.

The night demon was getting worse. He found he could barely sleep at all. Sometimes he thought the only things keeping him from losing it completely were physical work, his martial arts, and his determination to win Nila body and soul.

Yet he wasn't sure how much longer he could get through the night without her.

• • •

Saturday evening Nila had just finished dressing for her date with Jake when the doorbell chimed. She checked herself in the cheval mirror, and decided her straight black skirt, white silk blouse, and waist-length black velvet jacket was just right for an evening of dining and dancing at the country club.

She heard the doorbell chime again and hurried downstairs. It secretly amused her that Jake thought nothing of running in and out of her house all day, but at night he always waited to be invited in. Not once had he used the key she had given him. The man was a paradox.

"You're early—" she began as she flung open the door. Her smile faded along with everything else she intended to say as she stared at her visitor.

"Good evening, Nila," her ex-fiancé said. "I apologize for dropping in on you unannounced. I must speak to you, and I didn't think the telephone was appropriate for what I have to say. May I come in?"

She moistened her dry lips with her tongue. "Well, I suppose so. But just for a minute or two. I have plans for the evening."

"Thank you. You look lovely, by the way." He kissed the air near her temple as he moved past her.

Nila closed the door. Why he had come to see her? And why had she never really noticed he was an air kisser?

She led him into the sitting room and sat down on the sofa immediately, knowing his sense of courtliness required him to stand until she was seated. "What is it you have to say, Frank?"

"This is difficult for me," he said, continuing to

stand in the middle of the room. "I feel like a heel. I don't want you to think, ummmm . . ."

He was babbling, Nila thought. Very unusual for him. Frank was always precise in speech, manners, and habits, as precise as the crease in his pants.

". . . ummmm, I just got home this afternoon. On the plane, I planned what I was going to say, but now it seems all wrong. I hope you'll be patient with me while I find the right words."

Nonplussed and slightly irritated, Nila leaned back and waited.

Frank locked his hands behind his back. Deep in thought, he paced over the Oriental carpet.

Nila watched him and counted. He took five steps one way, turned, and took five steps in the other direction. Oddly, his precision was one of the things that had first attracted her to Frank. That and his respectable predictability.

It certainly hadn't been his appearance. He wasn't irresistibly attractive, though he was pleasant enough in a mild sort of way. He looked older than his thirty-two years, with his salt-and-pepper hair beginning to thin on top. He did have a nice gray eyes and a confident smile.

"Frank, if you keep pacing like that, you'll wear a hole in my carpet," she said, not bothering to hide her irritation. "Don't worry about how you're going to say whatever it is. Just say it."

He stopped and smiled at her. "You're so sweet and understanding." The sincerity in his voice made her force back a chuckle. Her annoyance hadn't even registered with him. "You always know how to put me at ease. That's one of the things I love about you."

She stared hard at him.

"I didn't know what a jewel you were until . . .

ummmm, well, you know." He sat down on the sofa beside her. "I've come to beg your forgiveness for being such a fool."

Apprehension and dread flooded through Nila. She didn't like the way this was going at all. "Well, there's no need to do that. I know love can make people do crazy things." Boy, did she ever!

"It wasn't love, Nila." He shook his head. "It was just one of those things. Maybe an early mid-life crisis." He straightened his shoulders. "But it's over now."

She slanted a quick, uncertain glance at him, wondering what was coming next. "I'm sorry to hear that."

"So sweet," he murmured fondly. "I knew you'd understand. When Tina and I realized our marriage was a dreadful mésalliance, we parted company. Tina's a lovely girl and a great secretary, but—"

"Good heavens!" Nila exclaimed. "You don't mean to tell me you just left the poor woman in Niagara Falls?"

Frank looked offended. "Of course not. I put her on a plane to Reno. She's going to start divorce proceedings there. I'll pay for her living expenses and the divorce. One must pay for one's mistakes. But I hope you won't make me pay too dearly." He snaked his arm behind her on the top of the sofa.

Nila shifted away from him, sitting on the edge of the cushion. "I don't bear you any ill will, Frank. I'm sorry things didn't work out for you. But—"

He leaped to his feet. "You're an angel!"

To her astonishment, he then got down on one knee in front of her and took her hands in his.

"Frank, have you lost your mind? What do you think you're doing?"

"Begging you to take me back." He lifted her

hands and kissed them. "I didn't know what a good thing I had until I almost threw it away. We're perfectly suited, you and I. I know we can pick up where we left off."

"The only thing Nila will be picking up," came a low, deadly voice, "is the pieces after I get through with you. Unless you have a death wish, I strongly advise you to take your hands off my woman."

Nine

A stunned silence followed the threat.

Nila's gaze flew to Jake. He eclipsed the doorway, looking larger than life, an angry demigod elevated from mere mortal status by his power and fury. The ruby in his earlobe glowed bloodred in the light. Standing there in his dark tailored suit, he could have been carved in granite. His expression was the coldest, most dangerous one she'd ever seen on any human face.

Frank's bewildered gaze traveled from Jake to Nila and back again. His grip on her hands tightened.

Of all the times for Jake to walk in uninvited, Nila thought wildly, why now? Then she went brain-dead as she stared at five-feet-eleven-inches of virile male hostility. She tried to free her hands, but Frank held on.

He also found his voice first. "I don't know who you are, mister, but you've got a lot of nerve claiming my fiancée is your woman. Get out of here or I will call the police."

Nila sucked in enough air to speak. "Oh Lord!

Not the police again." At last she pulled her hands free.

"Do you know this man, Nila?" Frank demanded, still down on one knee.

"Yes, this is Jake Madison. He's my . . . house-guest. Jake, this is Frank Tate. He used to be my fiancé."

The two men regarded each other with undisguised animosity.

"I'm her lover," Jake said in the same menacing tone in which he'd issued his threat.

"What!" Frank stood up.

Nila felt the blood drain from her face. She glared at Jake in seething silence.

"You've slept with this cretin?" Frank asked her.

She ignored him as she jumped to her feet. Hands curling into fists, she took a couple of steps toward Jake, then stopped. "One night in bed doesn't make you my lover."

"The hell it doesn't," he growled.

Frank yelled indignantly, "You never slept with me, and we were engaged!"

"Shut up, Frank." She kept her furious gaze on Jake as he stepped into the room.

His gaze left her and settled on the man behind her. "Nila gave herself to me. She knows she belongs to me. She's just having a little trouble keeping up her end of the commitment. You have one minute to get out of her house and out of her life."

"She doesn't belong to you," Frank said. "I was here before you and I'll be here long after you're gone, buddy. *You* get out or I'll be forced to punch you in the nose."

"Thirty seconds." Jake stood as indifferent as a stone.

Appalled, Nila stepped between the men. "Stop talking about me like I'm not here. Jake, go into the kitchen and wait for me. I'll straighten everything out, and then we'll talk."

No one was more surprised than she when Jake simply lifted her off her feet and set her behind him.

"That does it." Frank shoved the sleeves of his cashmere up to his elbows. "I don't want to get violent, but you're asking for it."

Seriously alarmed, Nila shouted, "Don't you dare try to hit him, Frank! He's a martial arts expert. He'll wipe the floor with your face."

She jumped between them again. "I've had enough of this. I will not tolerate such juvenile behavior."

Turning a hard look on Jake, she said, "You don't understand what's going on here. It has nothing to do with you."

"Everything you do is my business. You belong to me."

"He keeps saying that." Frank sounded confused and a bit petulant. "Nila, tell him to stop saying that."

"Shut up, Frank," they both said.

"Behave yourself, Jake." She poked him in the chest with her index finger. "If you so much as *look* like you're going to hit this man, I'll never speak to you again as long as I live."

She whipped around to face her ex-fiancé. Bewilderment filled his eyes. "Our engagement ended when you eloped with Tina. But no matter how or why our engagement ended, it was the right thing for both of us. It should never have happened at all. I don't love you, Frank. I never did. I'm sorry."

Frank dropped his gaze, shifting uncomfortably from one foot to the other.

Nila softened her tone. "Be honest with yourself. You know you never loved me either. We've been friends for a long time." She smiled when he glanced up at her again. "We were two old stick-in-the-mud single people who were tired of living alone in a married world. We became engaged because we needed someone, and we were comfortable together. That's all it was."

Frank looked thoughtful for a moment. "Friendship can be a good basis for marriage. We could have a nice life together."

"No!" Jake's voice cut through the room like a steel blade.

Nila shot him a warning glance over her shoulder. "I'm capable of speaking for myself." She dug her nails into her palms to control her temper as she continued talking to Frank. "I thought a marriage based on friendship would be enough for me, but I've discovered it isn't. I need more than that. Apparently you do, too, or you wouldn't have married Tina."

She reached out and gave his arm a maternal pat. "Go home now. Call her in Reno and try to work things out with her. Maybe the two of you just got cold feet because everything happened so fast."

Frank stared at her for a long moment, his eyes starting to shine with hope. "Do you really think she might give me another chance?"

"You won't know until you ask her. Go home. I wish you all the best."

He pulled his sweater sleeves down to his wrists. Casting several dubious looks at Jake, he moved toward the door, then he stopped and turned around. "I guess you're right about friendship not being enough. Maybe I always knew that too." He smiled. "As a friend, I'm here for you if you need me."

"She won't need you," Jake said without taking his eyes off Nila.

Nila sighed. Her head was beginning to hurt.

Tension filled the silence between her and Jake as Frank left. They heard the front door open, then close.

She spoke first in a clipped, icy tone. "Don't you ever humiliate me like that again."

"Nila—"

"Listen to me!" she cried, spinning out of his reach when he tried to touch her. She walked over to the fireplace.

"I'm getting a headache the size of Texas." She looked at him as she rubbed the back of her neck. His expression softened for the first time since he'd entered the room, and he took a step toward her.

"Stop right there," she ordered. To her surprise, he complied. "I'm very upset with you. You have no right to threaten a guest in my house. You have no right to barge in acting like a wild-eyed caveman, when you don't even know what's going on. What's the matter with you? Why would you do something so idiotic?"

The flame in Jake's eyes burned brighter. He shoved his hands into his trouser pockets as though he suddenly found it necessary to confine them. "Upset doesn't begin to describe how I'm feeling." His mouth twisted wryly. "I've respected your wishes to keep our relationship platonic until you say otherwise. I've done everything I can to win you but whistle the 'William Tell Overture' while standing on my head. And I'll do that, too, if that's what it takes."

He dragged in an angry breath. "So what do I

find when I walk in here tonight? Another man on his knees, holding your hands, *kissing* your hands. The two of you were so involved with each other, you didn't even hear me knocking on the door. How could you let him do that when you know you belong to me?"

That infuriated her all over again. "Dammit, Jake, I don't belong to you. I'm not a book. I'm not a piece of furniture. I'm not an object you can own. You can't win a woman like she was a lottery prize! I love you, but I sure as hell don't belong to you!" As soon as she blurted out that last statement, Nila squeezed her eyes shut. She couldn't have been more horrified if she'd just cut her throat with a rusty knife.

She heard Jake's sharp intake of breath, then a stirring sound. She supposed he was scrambling to find a chair. What did it mean when a man had to sit down after a woman declared her love for him? Nothing good, she feared.

"I wish I hadn't said that," she murmured, and opened her eyes.

He was sitting in a chair, looking stunned. Poleaxed right between the eyes. For the first time since they'd met, he didn't seem to know what to say or do. At last he asked quietly, "Did you mean that?"

She smiled weakly. "Yes, I meant it, and yes, I really wish I hadn't said it."

He rubbed his hand over his face. "This changes everything." His voice was so soft, she realized he was talking to himself, not to her.

"It changes nothing."

"Sit down, sweetheart." He smiled. "We need to talk about this."

She shook her head. "Not tonight. I feel like a blacksmith is pounding an anvil inside my head.

I've had all I can take. Please leave. I can't go out with you tonight."

She crossed the room and walked out the door, managing not to stumble though her legs felt weak and shaky. Her heels tapped against the hardwood floor, breaking the stillness of the hall-way. She made it to the stairs before she heard him follow.

She resisted the urge to run. Instead, she waited on the fourth step, holding onto the bannister. When she heard him nearing, she turned and slanted a reproachful glance in his direction.

"What now, Jake?" Her voice came out as a weary sigh.

He stood at the bottom of the stairs, regarding her steadily. What emotion, she wondered, caused him to look at her so oddly?

"Say it again," he said. "You know, how you feel . . . about me."

She blinked, more than a little surprised by his almost humble request. "I love you."

"I knew we belonged together the first time I saw you." He looked at her with such need and long-ing, she could have wept.

She closed her eyes. "Please leave now. I need time alone."

"Good night, sweetheart."

She listened to the sound of his footsteps echo-ing back down the hall. When she opened her eyes, he was gone.

Nila woke from a bad dream in which Jake had turned into sand as soon as she said she loved him. The sand had been swiftly carried away by a rainstorm.

Rain, a pounding rain. No, that was wrong. She

raised up on elbow. Disoriented and not quite awake, she realized it was raining. Rain was drumming hollowly on the roof, but the pounding came from downstairs.

She peered at the digital clock on the table beside the bed. Who could be hammering on her back door at two A.M.?

Feeling uneasy, she got up, put on a robe, and went downstairs.

In the kitchen she flipped on the overhead light, then the back porch light. "Who is it?" she called out in a high, nervous tone.

Relief rushed through her when Jake identified himself. She unlocked the door and threw it open.

He stood on the porch dripping wet, wearing only a pair of jeans. No shirt or jacket.

"Oh, Jake!" She wrapped her hand around his bare arm. His skin was so cold. "Come in." She drew him into the room and shut the door against a draft of damp, chilly air.

She was alarmed by his condition. He was frighteningly pale and haggard. His chest heaved as though he couldn't catch his breath. And his eyes— She shuddered. His eyes were black and tortured.

Something was terribly wrong.

"Are you ill?" Her worried gaze traveled over him. She touched his forehead, stroked his jaw.

"Can't sleep," he mumbled.

"Wait here. I'll get towels and a blanket."

He gripped her arm weakly and fixed her with an intense, almost fearful gaze. *"Nila."*

"What is it, Jake?" The haunted look in his eyes unsettled her. "What's wrong?"

His hand fell away from her arm. His gaze shifted out of focus. "Can't sleep." He spoke in a low tone mixed with horror and despair. "Need you. Can't sleep anymore without you. I need you to lie down with me. *Please*."

A whirlpool of emotions churned inside her. Something was wrong, and whatever it was, it was eating him alive.

"All right, Jake," she said gently. "But first we have to get you dry and warm. Come with me."

She led him into the downstairs bathroom. There she helped him strip off his wet jeans and shoved him into a warm shower.

A short while later, she wrapped a blanket around his shoulders and took him back to the kitchen. He slumped into a chair at the table while she put water on for tea.

She kept glancing worriedly at him as she rummaged through cabinets. Color was seeping back into his face, but the haunted look hadn't quite left his eyes.

"Take these," she said, handing him a glass of water and some tablets.

He frowned. "What's this? Don't need it."

"Indulge me. It's just vitamin C and aspirin. I don't want you to get sick."

"Okay." He swallowed the pills with a mouthful of water.

"Why didn't you use the key I gave you instead of standing around in the freezing rain?" she asked, pulling out a chair for herself.

"Didn't want to betray your trust." He lowered his head. Hair fell into his eyes, and he combed it back with his fingers.

"That's the silliest thing I've ever heard you say. I'd much rather you use your key than have you catch pneumonia." She got up and fixed their tea.

"What's wrong, Jake?" she asked, coming back to the table with two mugs. "Why can't you sleep?"

"Nightmares." He took in a deep, shuddery breath

and wrapped both hands around the steaming cup of tea.

She thought of the dream that had woken her. Jake turning to sand and being swept away by rain. "Tell me about it," she said softly.

Jake felt the darkness rise up inside him. His heart hammered against his ribs. The darkness had driven him from the cottage and through the rain to seek the one person he hoped could make it go away.

He shifted his gaze to Nila. She looked like purity personified in a fluffy white robe. Beneath it he caught glimpses of a long white nightgown. Eyelet lace with pink satin ribbons edged the neckline, hem, and cuffs.

So pretty and so clean. He didn't want the dark thing to touch her. —

But he *was* the darkness.

He could lie with her for a thousand years and *it* would always be there waiting, because in some strange way, he was afraid to let it go.

He closed his eyes. "I thought it was just the nightmare. But it isn't. I'm afraid it's more."

"You afraid? Why, I bet bullets bounce right off you. You're never afraid." Her voice was light and teasing.

He opened his eyes. Her gentle smile warmed him. "People who show fear are easy targets. I know fear and I know how not to show it. In a minute I'm going to tell you a story about being afraid. Get ready to have your superman illusions shattered."

She placed her hand on his as though to assure him that nothing he could say would shatter her image of him, of his strength and courage.

"I think it really started with Vic, my adoptive father." He turned his hand over and felt her fingers twine with us. "Vic wasn't a young man when we met. His wife—the greatest love of his life, he called her—had been dead for many years, and they had no children. Vic was a good man. Disciplined but kind. Strong but gentle. He made a modest living teaching martial arts, and he was satisfied that he was doing something worthwhile. Vic instilled his love for justice in me. He was the first person who ever believed in me, believed I could do something with my life that would make a difference in the world."

"I wish I could have met him."

Jake smiled faintly and closed his eyes again. "Vic was murdered." He heard her sharp intake of breath. "He tried to stop a sixteen-year-old kid from mugging an old woman. The kid had a knife and a system full of drugs. He was flying too high to even feel pain. They told me it took four men to take him down.

"I was in college at the time, studying criminal justice, aiming to be a lawyer. I went crazy when they told me what happened. At first I hated that kid. Then I hated the drugs that turned a teenage boy into a killer. And I hated the people who had sold that poison to him."

He remained silent with his eyes shut tight for a long moment.

Nila ached for him. They did indeed have more in common than appeared on the surface. She still felt the hurt from being abandoned by her father. He still felt the rage over his own father's sense-less, violent death.

She squeezed his hand, letting him feel the solidity of her presence. And she waited, fearing what was to come.

Windblown rain rattled the windowpanes and gurgled loudly through a downspout beyond the back door. Rain cleansed the earth. Nila prayed the sharing of whatever haunted him would be cleansing too.

When he spoke again, his voice was curiously void of emotion. "After I graduated, I was hired by the DEA." He opened his eyes and met her gaze. "I went into undercover with the cold, hard heart of an avenger. It didn't take me long to earn a reputation for being a fearless bastard who would go into situations no one else would." A humorless smile tipped the corners of his mouth. "My DEA friends nicknamed me 'Mad Man Madison.'"

He released her hand, picked up his mug of tea, and took a sip. "I thrived on the danger. I lived it and breathed it until I was nothing but the job." His face became taut, as if every muscle had tightened. A fine sheen of sweat glistened upon his brow. "I frigging loved it, and I told myself it was because I was making a difference just like Vic taught me. Every dealer I took down, no matter how petty, was a gift to Vic. But it was like trying to empty the ocean one teaspoon at a time." Bitterness hardened his voice. "Take one player out of the game and a dozen more showed up to fill the void.

"Something was dying inside me, and something dark was growing in its place. I could feel it happening, but I didn't know how to stop it. So I tried to ignore it. I buried myself in the job because that's all I had, that's all I was." He spoke now with a passion that was taking its toll on him. The semicircles of fatigue beneath his eyes appeared to grow darker.

Nila wanted to stop him. She should order him to rest. But she didn't because she knew he wouldn't allow her to stop him, and because he seemed to need her to listen to what he had to say.

His eyes took on a feverish glow, and his hands trembled on the mug. "Three weeks before I met you, one of my string of informants set up a buy for me with a man who called himself 'the Hammer.'" The deadly shark smile formed on Jake's lips. It sent a chill racing up Nila's spine. "His real name was Don Shea. He was nothing more than a sleazy street-level pusher, but he was rumored to be well connected to the money men up the chain. My intention was to bust Shea and flip him."

"What does that mean? Flip him?"

Jake rubbed his face. "Turn him into an informant. Get him to give us information and introductions to the movers and shakers up the chain.

"I met Shea alone in the back room of a seedy bar. Rae and another agent were waiting outside in the car for the deal to go down. They were supposed to bust Shea and me with him so my cover wouldn't be blown.

"It was a situation I'd been in hundreds of times. At first Shea didn't seem any different from any of the other scum I've known. I was stringing him along. The deal was going down just as planned. Then for some reason I still can't understand, I got this feeling my scam was blown. Shea started talking and acting crazy. I realized this guy was a psycho. I started to walk away, but it was too late."

Nila felt the room closing in on her.

"Too late." He leaned forward, his elbows on the table, his head in his still-trembling hands. "Too late because Shea had taken a gun out of his pocket. It was pointed at my chest. The SOB *smiled* at me." He spoke in a tone of horror mixed with rage. "For a fragment of eternity, I stared death in the face. I couldn't move. Shea pulled the trigger. I heard a click. Nothing happened. The weapon had jammed."

He shook his head as though he still couldn't believe it. His feverish gaze came to rest upon her face, but she knew he wasn't really seeing her. He was replaying the incident in his mind, and in his eyes she saw it all—the unspeakable terror of believing he was going to die and the incredible miracle that he didn't.

Fingers of fear and anger wove through her as she realized how very close to death he had come. They never would have met. In that instant, Jake became infinitely more precious to her. It no longer mattered whether he loved her or not. She had enough love for both of them.

"We stared at each other." Jake began to speak rapidly, his hands gesturing wildly. "Then I went crazy. I knocked the gun out of Shea's hand. Grabbed the front of his shirt. I was bouncing him around. He was screaming. I was screaming, spewing out threats and abuse. Then I was reaching for my own weapon. I slammed Shea against the wall, and he found himself staring down the barrel of my gun."

Cold seeped through Nila's skin and chilled her to the bone. She seized one of Jake's hands, bracing herself for whatever was to come.

He hung on to her hand as though it were the only thing keeping him from flying apart. "I could smell Shea's fear and I could see the caldron of madness and hatred in his eyes. And he could smell and see mine. For a minute, I knew I was as crazy as that psycho. It scared me so bad, I started to shake.

"I didn't kill him. But I *wanted* to," Jake whispered hoarsely. "That's when I knew the job was over for me. I had almost crossed a line no human being should cross. That's the nightmare that wakes me up every night. I see myself with the gun in my hand, my finger tightening on the trigger, and I feel myself getting closer and closer to slipping over the razor's edge. It's like there's this dark place in my soul, and it just keeps getting bigger and darker. I can't sleep at all now."

He tilted his head and gazed at her intently. "The only time I didn't have the nightmare was the night I spent with you. I don't think I'll ever sleep again if you're not with me."

Nila felt his pain deeply. Words of comfort swirled in her mind, but they were inadequate. None of them could heal the dark place inside him. Only he could heal himself. But if he believed she could keep the night terrors away, then she would believe it too.

"I love you," she said quietly.

Jake stared at the beautiful woman who loved him. She had spoken those words first in anger, then as though she were resigned to a fate she wasn't certain she wanted. Now she spoke them with such eloquence, he nearly cried.

Some of the darkness faded from him. Her love reached out to him, and like a ray of morning light passing through a windowpane, it began to shine upon his heart.

He wished he could say those words back to her. He couldn't, though, because that kind of intimacy scared the hell out of him. Yet from the first time their eyes had met in the casino, he had known they were two halves of a whole. Now he knew with absolute certainty his life had been spared for a reason.

That reason was Nila.

They needed each other.

For a while he sat holding her hand. He listened to the wind, the rain, the sound of his heartbeat.

At last he said, "I care deeply for you."

"I know."

His gaze searched her serenely smiling face. "More than you'll ever know."

"It's all right, Jake." She squeezed his hand. "I don't expect you to say you love me if you don't. My love for you is unconditional."

That troubled him. No one but Vic had ever given him that kind of unselfish love. *And one senseless act of violence had robbed him of it.*

Confusion and fear coursed through him. What if something happened to Nila? He shoved that unbearable thought away. Nothing would happen to her, he told himself. He wouldn't allow anything bad to happen to her. He vowed to protect her, keep her safe, until his last dying breath.

"Jake?" The apprehension endowed in that single word brought him back to the moment. "You're crushing my hand. Are you all right?"

"I'm sorry, sweetheart," he said, easing his grip on her. He lifted her hand to his mouth for a quick, regretful kiss, then lowered their joined hands back to the table.

He owed her an explanation for why he couldn't say he loved her. With a sigh, he began to try to explain something he wasn't sure he understood. "Nila, I don't know what love means to me anymore. It seems like I should love you." His voice sounded strange to him. It was full of emotions he couldn't sort out. "Maybe it's because I haven't let myself love anyone since Vic died. Hell, maybe I'm afraid to love anybody because—" He broke off, unable to finish the sentence because it seemed so irrational to him. "But if I don't know what it means to me, how can I say that I love you? It would just be words."

"Well, there's always time," she said. "Perhaps in time you'll know."

Her response surprised him. He hadn't expected her to set aside her own deeply ingrained fears of trusting men to reassure him. "Yes." He nodded, feeling oddly humbled. "There's always time."

He gazed at her for a long moment, then he said, "Until I can say those words to you and mean them heart and soul, you will have my deepest respect and loyalty. No one will care for you more than I. You will be the center of my existence."

"I've never been the center of anyone's existence before." A dazzling smile lit up her face, and his senses swam in its brilliance.

She rose to her feet. "There's been enough talk for tonight. But I want you to know you're not as bad as you think you are. You're an honorable man, Jake. You could have killed Shea, but you didn't because you value human life. You could have told me what I wanted to hear, but you didn't because you're not a liar. No matter what you believe, the job you did made a difference to thousands of people you will never know. You've made a difference in my life too."

Another shaft of light warmed the dark corners of his heart.

"Come to bed now," she ordered softly, tugging on his hand.

Ten

Jake sank down on the edge of Nila's bed. He was naked, having abandoned the blanket during a passionate kiss on the stairs.

His gaze traveled over the lace curtains, over the feminine things laid out on her dresser, over the walls with their rosebuds forever waiting to unfold their petals. He had imagined himself here so many times.

He shifted his gaze to Nila as she slipped out of her robe. She turned to look at him. Her eyes shone with love, passion, anticipation. It took his breath away.

Her fingers found the row of buttons on her nightgown. As he watched her undress, he was struck by the realization that she no longer reminded him of the tightly closed rosebuds on her wall. She was letting go of her fears, leaving behind her old self, risking the future. He felt awed by her tremendous courage to love without knowing whether she would ever be loved in return.

A disconcerting thought snaked through his

mind. A part of him was as tightly closed as those rosebuds. Regret filled him. He didn't want to be that way. But change was hard, even when change was desperately wanted.

She smiled at him. The desire and longing in that smile erased his uneasy thoughts. His heart beat faster.

"Come here, sweetheart." He held out his hand. "Come let me *show* you how I feel about you."

Wordlessly, she came to stand in front of him. Her half-unbuttoned gown revealed the ivory column of her throat and the inviting slopes of her breasts.

He placed his hands on her hips, drawing her to him until she stood between his thighs. He stared long into her face, wanting to commit to memory the picture of the woman to whom he had disclosed the dark secrets of his life.

"I've been needing you so badly." His arms slid around her, and he rested his forehead upon her midriff. The warmth of her body penetrated through the thin cotton of her nightgown. He breathed in the scent of her aroma mixed with the exotic island perfume.

"I need you too," she whispered.

Overcome by the love and tenderness in her voice, Jake squeezed his eyes shut. He felt her touch the back of his head, then her hands trailed over his naked shoulders and down his arms.

Desire came as a welcome song. He lowered his head and moved his mouth across the white fabric covering her stomach.

"I love you," she whispered. She bent down to surround him in a feverish embrace. "I don't think I ever really lived until I met you." Her lips touched his hair.

For a moment, he could only hold her close.

Then he said, "Words have always come easy to me."

She straightened. He lifted his head and met her questioning gaze.

"I learned to use words to play on the emotions of others. I've used them to get into and out of all sorts of situations. I've used glib, meaningless words to manipulate people into doing whatever I wanted them to do." His smile was strained. "Now I can't find the words to express my feelings for you."

"You don't have to say anything," she said, smoothing back his hair.

"I know. But I want to." He began working on the remaining buttons of her nightgown, with care and trembling fingers. "When you walked into the casino, you took my breath away. I couldn't resist seeking you out. I stood for the longest time just watching you play the slot machine, trying to figure you out, trying to understand what drew me to you. Your decency was a part of it. I could see it shining in your eyes along with the sweetness of your soul. I was thirsty for that sweetness and your compassion, which is so richly you, for in my world I had seen little sweetness or compassion.

"Since I've been here, I've come to understand that you are an anchor, Nila. You anchor your family and friends. Maybe that's another thing I sensed in you the first time I saw you. Maybe I need you to be my anchor too."

"Oh, Jake, I'll be anything you want me to be," she whispered, bending to kiss his brow.

"You are so beautiful." He parted her soft nightgown and kissed the swollen tip of her breast. Heat coiled deep within his body. Anything else he might have said to her was lost in the flames of that heat.

Hot. Her skin felt so hot beneath his fingers and mouth. He heard her repeating his name in a low, throaty moan. Her quivering body, the frantic movement of her hands on him told him that she, too, felt the white-hot heat burning between them.

"Nila!" Blood pounded in his ears. It had been much too long. He couldn't wait another moment.

Together they shoved the gown off her shoulders, down her arms, past her hips. Then he was lowering himself backward onto the bed, pulling her on top of him.

Jake fused his mouth with hers, hungrily claiming, affirming his need for her. She was everything that made a man feel strong and tender all at once. He trailed his hands along the enticing curve of her waist and hips, reveling in the satiny feel of her skin.

The sweetness of having her tongue explore, taste, and tease the inside of his mouth ignited flames that blazed through his veins. She was his, holding back nothing, giving everything she had. That she should give herself so completely filled him with reverence, a reverence that revealed itself in his touch.

Tremors wracked her body. She twisted and writhed over him, heightening his arousal. Her ardor made him hungrier, pushing him to the edge of reason.

Nila tore her mouth away from his to look into his eyes. Her heart overflowed with love for him. She wove her fingers into the dark, silky tresses spread out on her bed. Her legs moved, rubbing against the hard roughness of his thighs.

He rolled her over to the center of the bed, covering her with his body, taking her mouth again with a kiss that grew more demanding, more enticing, more out of control. Everywhere he touched her she burned. Burned until she could bear it no longer.

Nila broke the contact of their lips to scorch kisses down his throat. His husky groan excited her to the edge of madness. She wiggled restlessly against him, pushing at his shoulders until he rolled onto his back again.

She rose over him, spreading one thigh across his while dampening his flat nipples with kisses. The primitive, passionate woman she was seemed insatiable as she explored his body with her hands and mouth.

The feel of his hands on her breasts drove her to peaks of pleasure so intense, she cried out. Thrusting her lower body against his, she communicated her readiness and need.

She whispered endearments as she moved over him and joined their bodies together. Desire raged, becoming a frenzied obsession for fulfillment. Tension spiraled inside her as they rocked in an age-old rhythm.

His grip on her hips tightened as their lovemaking reached a shocking strength. She tensed against him as he thrust deeper. Waves of heat pushed her toward a climax. The force of it racked her from head to toe. She heard his guttural cry as he succumbed to his own ecstasy.

Nila collapsed over him. She lay there, too drained to move, listening to the beat of his heart and the ragged sound of his breathing. Then she became aware of his hands—such marvelous hands!—gliding over her back.

She raised her head to look at him. His eyes were half closed. A soft smile rested upon his lips.

"Sleep, my love," she said, easing away from him.

"Don't go," he sighed, completely closing his eyes.

"I won't leave you." She reached over him to turn out the light. After drawing the bed linens over them both, she cuddled close to his warm, damp body. "I'll be with you," she whispered. "I love you."

He murmured something and slid his arm over her breasts. She knew he was already well on his way to a deep slumber.

Outside, rain still fell in a ceaseless, lulling rhythm. She lay awake for perhaps an hour, holding Jake close, thinking of the transformation he had wrought upon her life, and praying she could work the same miracle upon his.

Morning came. Jake awoke to find the sun's rays filtering through the lace curtains. He stretched, feeling rested and peaceful from a sleep untroubled by night demons.

Beside him he felt Nila stir, instinctively seeking his warmth. He rolled onto his side, propped his head upon his arm, and gazed at her face. Waking up with a lover had always made him uncomfortable. But waking up to find Nila curled up against him was a pleasure so rich, he couldn't begin to describe it.

She loved him. Knowing that filled him with overwhelming emotions. Although he liked the idea of her being in love with him, the feelings it evoked in him were new and perplexing. He cared for her in ways he'd never cared for a woman before. But was that love?

Her eyes fluttered open. A beautiful rosy blush spread across her face as she met his intense gaze. "Good morning," she said shyly.

"Good morning." He brushed a kiss across her lips.

"You look rested."

He smiled and without another word made love to her with infinite tenderness.

Over the next few days, Jake slowly became aware of the healing process going on within him. Through Nila's loving eyes he began to see and accept himself as a good man, a man who still had dark thoughts and selfish motives at times, but nevertheless a good man. It was a sign of maturity, one that he knew Vic would have been proud of, and it wasn't such a bad thing.

The nightmare was gone too. He slept through each night with Nila's soft, sweet body next to his, and when he woke each morning, he felt more at peace with himself than he could ever remember.

Love and happiness were sneaking up on him in little ways. In Nila's thoughtfulness, in her willingness to give unselfishly, in the sexy gleam in her brown-gold eyes, in her sweet smile, in the touch of her hand, in the endless empathy and understanding she gave to him as well as to the other people milling around in her universe.

In coming to terms with himself, Jake unconsciously opened his heart to the possibilities of loving her.

Two days before Thanksgiving, Jake sat on a practice mat laid out on the floor of the living room in the guest cottage, waiting for Miles. He'd moved their aikido lessons indoors, since the weather was growing colder.

Miles was late, an event even more rare than the boy's smiles. Feeling concerned, Jake finally left the cottage to look for him.

A few minutes later, he entered Nila's shop. She was alone and talking to someone on the phone. She hardly glanced up as he approached her.

She looked thunderstruck when she hung up a minute later. "That was my mother. She and Tolly really are coming home for the holidays. And she can't wait to meet you."

"Ah, so you told her about us?"

Nila nodded absently, her mind obviously still going over the conversation with her wayward parent.

"Was she upset that we're living together?"

"No." She smiled ruefully. "She's thrilled out of her mind. For the first time, I think she thinks we finally have something in common. You know the old adage about the apple not falling far from the tree? I think Mama is pleased that my apple finally fell."

Jake couldn't help laughing at her bemused expression.

She shot him an annoyed look. "You won't think it's so funny when Attila-the-Mom steamrolls right over you."

"Where's Angie?" he asked, deciding a change in subject might be wise.

"She had a conference with Miles's teacher and the school counselor."

Jake frowned. "Is Miles with her?"

"No, he's outside sitting in the gazebo, I think."

He came around the counter and kissed her. "Don't worry about Emma steamrolling me. We're going to get along just fine."

Nila hugged him. "I hope so."

"I'm going out to talk to Miles." He kissed the tip of her nose, then winked at her. "What do you say we meet back here after closing time? We can turn off the lights and do it on the floor behind this counter."

Her eyes widened and her cheeks flamed, but he could see she found his suggestion intriguing. "Get out of here, you pervert," she said with a laugh and tiny slap on his shoulder.

Jake grinned and headed for the veranda.

He found Miles in the gazebo, perched on the handrail. Sugar Booger snoozed on the floor beneath the boy's dangling feet.

"Hello, Jake," the boy said, not taking his eyes off a small spider hanging from the end of the gossamer dragline it was weaving into its web.

"Hi." Jake leaned against the handrail beside the little boy. As he glanced down at the lazy cat, Sugar Booger opened one eye, twitched his tail, then returned to his nap. "I was disappointed that you didn't come by for your aikido lesson."

"I did not feel up to the task today," Miles said, keeping watch on the spider's progress.

Jake didn't say anything for a moment as he studied the dejected look on Miles's face. Finally, he said, "You look like you could sing the blues."

"My voice isn't suited to singing the blues. It's too squeaky."

Jake forced back a chuckle. "What I meant is you look unhappy. It was an invitation to share your troubles."

Miles turned his head and met Jake's gaze. "The counselor at school believes I should advance to the fourth grade because second-grade work isn't challenging enough for me. My mother does not think it would be a sensible move at this time. She—" The boy frowned. "Mother says it is more important for me to interact with children my own age."

"What do you think?"

He shrugged his thin shoulders. "It makes no difference to me," he said, but Jake could sense that it did indeed make a difference to him. "The children in my class have no interest in being friends with me. They think I am a nerd." The boy paused to readjust his glasses on his long nose. "They hate me."

"What do you think of them?"

"I consider them . . ." He could see Miles searching his little computer brain for a descriptive word that wouldn't get him into hot water with an adult. "I think they are deadheads."

"Well then, hate 'em back," Jake said solemnly.

The boy's shocked expression clearly revealed that that was not the kind of advice he'd expected from a mature, reasonably intelligent adult. His mouth pursed in disapproval. "My mother says it's wrong to hate people even if they're mean and deserve it."

Jake smiled.

The owlish eyes behind thick-lensed glasses examined him carefully. Jake kept smiling. Those eyes went flicker-blink, flicker-blink, flicker-blink like a flashing blue strobe light. "Oh," he said at last. "That was a joke. You are teasing me."

"Yes." Jake nodded. "I am."

"Well, that's very amusing. Unfortunately, it doesn't solve my problem."

Jake laughed. "Lighten up, kid," he said, ruffling the boy's unruly blond hair. "I doubt that they really hate you. As you say, you're very smart. So I think you can answer this question. What makes one person become friends with another person?"

That set Miles's eyes flicker-blinking again. "Spiders I understand. But human beings are a complete mystery to me." He sighed heavily and rubbed the side of his nose as he thought it over. "Is it because those two people like the same things?" he asked hesitantly.

Jake nodded. "You know people better than you think. One person becomes friends with another because they have something in common. Maybe they both like scary movies, or playing football, or collecting stamps. What do you like that some of the kids in your class might like too?"

Miles brightened. "Chip Smith appeared to be particularly interested when I gave a report on tarantulas last week. He didn't believe I actually have one at home."

"That's a start. Why not invite Chip over to your house to see it?"

Miles looked skeptical.

"The worst thing that could happen is that he could say no," Jake said. "So what if he does? Big deal. It's his loss, not yours. Can you think of anything else the other kids might like?"

"Aikido!" One of the child's rare smiles warmed Jake's heart.

The next morning Jake received permission to give an aikido demonstration to Miles's second-grade class. It was a big success. He wasn't certain who the children viewed as the hero of the venture, himself or Miles, who had assisted him in showing the kids the various techniques of rolling and leaping falls.

He left the school knowing his prize aikido student would soon have more friends than he ever dreamed of.

That was also the day Jake discovered what he wanted to do with the rest of his life—teach aikido. He enjoyed working with children. If he had his own dojo in which to teach them, he could pass along the lessons Vic Madison had taught him.

• • •

"Maybe I should wear a suit," Jake said, scowling at his reflection in Nila's bedroom mirror on Thanksgiving morning.

"Whatever for?" she asked, slipping on a lush cranberry velvet dress with an ivory lace collar. She watched him fuss with his clothing. "You look just fine." And very handsome, she added silently. He wore conservative dark trousers with a white shirt and a beautiful new teal, rust, and wine cotton sweater.

Frowning, he smoothed his hand over his hair. "Maybe I should have it cut. What about the earring? Should I leave it at home?"

"I've never seen you act so nervous," she said, walking over to him. "Zip me up." She turned her back and lifted her hair away from her neck.

"Today is very important," he said, giving her nape a kiss before performing the intimate little task of zipping her dress. "What if I don't fit in?"

She twisted her head around and gave him an amused glance. "Aren't you the man who told me I shouldn't worry about other people's opinions?"

"Why do women always remember every little thing a man says?" he asked with mock severity. "Ten years later, a woman can recall something stupid a man once said to her and rub his nose in it."

"It's because we love you silly creatures." She turned and wrapped her arms around his waist. "Relax, we're just going to Clover's house. Angie and Miles will be there. Just family."

"But your mother will be there, too, and a lot of other people. First impressions are important, you know."

She laughed and hugged him. "Forget the suit.

Mama will *adore* the earring. I love you just the way you are, and so will everyone else."

"Why don't we stay home and make love?"

Nila forced herself not to respond to the wicked gleam in his dangerous eyes. "No way, José. If we don't show up at Clover's house, my mama will come looking for us. She still has a key. Do you really want her to catch us in bed?"

He looked thoughtful for a moment. "Would she insist on a shotgun wedding?" he asked hopefully.

Nila sighed. Did he still want to marry her? He hadn't brought up the subject since the day he'd sort of proposed to her in her kitchen. Marriage and babies had been on her mind ever since he'd moved in with her.

"No," she answered dismally. "It isn't Mama's style. She would probably act like it was a slumber party. I can just see her kicking off her shoes and settling down on the bed for a cozy conversation."

He grinned and shook his head. "I can't wait to meet Emma."

Two hours later, Nila stood in the far corner of Clover's formal parlor, listening to a friend's trials and tribulations of newfound parenthood. Thinking of babies made her think of Jake. She glanced across the room, seeking him out with her eyes, while murmuring appropriate comments when required.

Jake was engaged in a spirited discussion with the chief of police, the high school principal, and Clover's adult nephew—a blond Robert Redford type whose bit part in a made-for-television movie gave him star status in Danville—who was visiting from California.

Watching him, Nila smiled proudly. Jake need not have been concerned about fitting in. The man came alive in response to new situations and new people, and that aliveness drew people toward him. Children had followed him around like little lemmings, firing questions at him about martial arts. And Miles, to everyone's pleasant surprise, had been right with them, basking in Jake's praise of his aikido skills instead of hiding somewhere with his nose in a book. Nila had seen Angie's misty-eyed expression of joy as her son followed the other children when their parents finally shooed them off to another room to play.

Suddenly, Jake looked her way. The warmth in his eyes and his smile was so intimate, she wished they had stayed home to make love. More than ever, she knew he was the answer to all her frustrated yearnings and unfulfilled desires.

Heavenly days! What that man could do to her with a single scorching glance ought to be a federal offense.

She dropped her gaze and tuned back to the discussion of teething problems and the precious things that babies do.

Across the room, Jake entertained a moment's thought of grabbing Nila and finding a private spot where he could kiss her panty hose off. How long did Clover's Thanksgiving gathering go on?

As he returned his attention to the people surrounding him, he marveled over the way he had been accepted. Everyone he met had been cordial. Most people seemed fascinated by his DEA career, and several parents had approached him about giving their children martials arts training. His previous misgivings about fitting in with the people who inhabited Nila's world had faded, and he was having a wonderful time.

The group he was talking with broke up and scattered, leaving him alone with Will Heinrick, the high school principal. Will's wife, Jeannine, a lovely woman with a French-Canadian accent and an endless supply of ribald jokes, came over to join them. Jake had just accepted an invitation to speak to the high school student body on the subject of drug abuse, when an earsplitting shriek brought every conversation in the room to a halt.

A quick glance toward the door revealed the source of the scream. Jake saw a strikingly beautiful woman with dark hair permed into a halo around her face. He immediately recognized Nila's mother. Photographs didn't do her justice, he thought wryly. She was the kind of woman who instantly *owned* any space she happened to occupy. She also looked years younger than he had expected.

Emma Shepherd-Reeves-Nelson let out another shriek. Half a dozen bracelets slid toward her right elbow as she raised her arms high above her head. "My baby! My baby!" she cried out in what Jake took to be frenzied delight. People quickly moved out of her path as she blitzed through the room, doing a ridiculously sexy little touchdown dance all the way.

"Quick! Hide the lamp shades," he heard Jeannine say. "Emma has arrived." Her husband made a hushing noise, but ruined its effect by chuckling.

Jake grinned too. He got a glimpse of Nila's face just before her mother threw her arms around her. She had looked as though she didn't know whether to laugh or slither under the rug. Now her face was buried in the profusion of white and black feathers that were stitched on one shoulder of Emma's plunging V-neck, mini-length whorehouse-red sweater-dress. He wondered why Nila had neglected to tell him Emma and Angie frequented the same bizarre clothing shops.

He traded a smile with the Heinricks and excused himself, heading for the Sheperd ladies.

"My baby! My baby!" Emma exclaimed again, wildly rocking Nila from side to side.

A man—Tolly, Jake presumed—had trailed after Emma. He was as Nila had described him, a big, huggable teddy bear of a man. His smile seemed to stretch from ear to ear, and his blue eyes were apparently on permanent twinkle duty.

Jake watched him raise the camera he had slung around his neck. Firing off shot after shot, the man circled and bounced around the two women as though the mother-daughter reunion was the ultimate Kodak moment of a lifetime.

Nila sneezed. Jake's grin widened as she coughed out a mouthful of feathers.

"Mama, I can't breathe," came her muffled voice.

"Oh, I'm sorry, sweetie." Emma let go, but captured Nila's chin in her hand. She swung around, taking her daughter's face with her. Nila had to follow it quickly so as not to fall.

"Tolly, get a shot of this face." She patted Nila's cheek with her other hand. "Isn't this a great face? Look at that bone structure." She released her hold on her daughter's chin and tapped her between the shoulder blades. "Stand up straight. Bad posture is most unattractive. Don't frown like that, honey. Frowning gives you wrinkles."

A wrinkle-producing frown settled upon Jake's features. If Nila had received such conflicting signals all during her youth, it wasn't difficult to understand why she lacked confidence in her own beauty. Criticisms mixed with compliments must have been hell on the self-esteem of a sensitive child.

Emma's gaze swept over her daughter. "Baby, where did you get this dress? It's sweet, but must you always dress so plainly?"

Nila laughed, but Jake could tell it covered some discomfort. She locked her hands together in front of her. "I thought you gave up trying to be my personal arbiter of fashion, Mama. It's good to see you. I can't wait to hear all about your trip."

Her attempt to steer a different conversational direction failed. Emma wagged a finger tipped with a long red-polished nail at her daughter. "With your face and figure, you could wear the most daring styles, baby."

"She has a style all her own," Jake said, stepping forward to slide his arm around Nila's waist. He found himself on the receiving end of two pairs of identical brown-gold eyes—Emma's filled with curiosity and Nila's with surprise and gratitude.

"Understated elegance suits her perfectly," he continued, smiling at the woman he'd gladly die for. "Put her in a flashy dress and what do you see? A flashy dress, not Nila. Put her in a refined, enchanting dress like this one and her beauty shines through."

Emma slanted a contrite glance at her daughter. "I'm sorry, baby. The gentleman is right. You always look beautiful in your own special way." She turned to Jake with a smile he'd seen on Nila's face a thousand times. "I'm Emma, Nila's mama. You must be Jake Madison. She didn't tell me what a devastatingly handsome man you are. Love the earring. I do so *adore* a man with enough brass to be interestingly different. Tolly, love, come meet my baby's significant other. He used to work for the DEA."

Emma's arrival changed the tone of the gathering. Jake noticed how she traveled from one cluster of folks to another, pumping up the volume and injecting new life into everyone. All assembled became more animated and noisier.

And as he watched her, Jake forgave Emma for her awkwardness in dealing with her daughter. Emma sparkled. She bubbled. She dazzled. She shone so bright, he decided she ought to come with a warning label: Beware! Put on shades before looking directly at this woman!

Immediately following the most incredible Thanksgiving dinner Jake had ever tried to eat his way through, Emma announced it was time for a sing-along. She plunked Nila down on the piano bench, then—to Jake's astonishment—Emma persuaded *Clover* to join her in a rowdy rendition of "Born to Be Wild." Then it took no inducement on their parts to get Angie to stand up with them for a little Motown sound. "Stop in the Name of Love" was sung gesture-perfect. Diana Ross and the Supremes would have been proud.

Clapping and whistling along with everyone else, Jake wondered where he'd gotten the absurd idea that small towns raised sedate and ultraconservative people.

When the entire gathering was warmed up and singing their hearts and lungs out, Emma sidled up to Jake, "Come with me, you darling man. We haven't had a chance for a cozy talk all day."

Eleven

Wondering what she was up to, Jake followed Emma out into the hall.

She sat down on the stairs, crossed her shapely legs, and patted the space beside her. "Sit down." She smiled. "It's okay, I don't bite."

"I don't believe I'd want to bet the farm on that one, Emma," he responded, only half teasing.

She tossed back her head and laughed delightedly. "Jake, you're a pistol. I already like you immensely. Sit your butt down. I have things to say to you."

He sat. Shoulder to shoulder, neither of them spoke for a long moment. The sound of Nila's fine hand upon the piano keys and dozens of voices infiltrated the hallway.

"I've never seen my baby in love before," Emma said, breaking their silence. "I wasn't sure I ever would. You've really knocked her prim little socks off."

She looked straight at him. "Do you understand her?"

"Yes, ma'am, I believe I do."

Emma held his gaze for moment. "Good. I think you'll do." Her expression clouded. Some of the fizz went out of her sparkle. "It's always been difficult for me and my youngest daughter. We run at different speeds. Now, Mary was easy because, unfortunately, she's just like me. We have the same strengths and weaknesses. I don't think Nila realizes it, but she's stronger than her sister and I." She smiled, and it was a sad one.

"Mary and I flit from one thing to another, searching, I guess, for that rainbow we're sure must be right around the next corner. Nila doesn't waste her time rushing to get around the next corner. Maybe it's because she knows the view won't make her any happier than the one she already sees. Maybe it's because she looks inward for happiness, not outward.

"I've made more than my share of mistakes. Nila has been my rock, sometimes more my parent than my child. If she suffered from my mistakes— and surely she has—she never let it show. She just went on about her life in her quiet way.

"I guess what I'm trying to say is this. More often than not I make a mess of things when I deal with my youngest daughter. Everything I say and do comes out all wrong. But I love her something fierce. Nila loves you. If you aren't good to my baby, you'll have me to deal with. Do we understand each other, Jake?"

"Yes, Emma, we certainly do."

"Good. Now, do you plan to marry my baby?"

"If she'll have me."

"And if she won't?"

He grinned. "We'll just have to keep living in sin, because I'm not giving her up. I found her and I'm keeping her as long as there's breath in my body."

"That's isn't the prettiest speech I've ever heard,

but it'll do." She smiled. Her radiance was back in full force. "And so will you." She rose. "Come along. Let's set this party on its ear. It's Miller time."

It was late in the evening when Nila and Jake left Clover's house. Before heading home, they took a stroll down Millionaire's Row, enjoying the chilly night air and sharing tidbits of thoughts and impressions about the day's events and the people Jake had met.

"I like Emma," he said. "She's quite a character. At one point, I decided she's a powerful witch. She casts a magical spell over everyone she comes in contact with."

Nila laughed. "I've yet to meet a person who doesn't like Emma. She's funny and outrageous. People tend to forgive her anything."

He stared at her for a moment. "Even you."

"Especially me."

"Would you consider leasing the cottage to me?"

It was her turn to stare at him. She swallowed thickly. "I thought you were happy living with me."

"I am." He squeezed her hand. "I don't want to live in it. Since this area is zoned for business, I want to open my own dojo. I'd have to make a few changes inside. Knock out the bedroom wall and open it up into one huge room, and—" He broke off when she came to sudden halt.

"I think that's a fine idea. You're a good teacher," she said, looking up at him. "I think you will also be in great demand as a consultant to local law enforcement agencies and school officials if you choose to do so. Vic would be as proud of you as I am." She didn't add that she was so thrilled she could hardly speak, because his plans meant he truly wanted to settle down with her.

Jake just smiled. Capturing her face between his hands, he kissed her. Then turning her around, he led her back home.

Within minutes of reaching home, Jake received a phone call from Rae Garcia.

"Amazon! How's it going?"

"I've been trying to reach you all day, Mad Man."

The cord of the wall-mounted phone stretched across the kitchen as Jake walked over to the window and stood looking out. "No, it's not too late," Nila heard him say, "and your hotel isn't far from here. You can be here in less than ten minutes." He gave her directions to Nila's house, then hung up.

"Guess what, sweetheart. That was Rae Garcia. She's been in town all day. If we had known she was coming, we could have taken her to Clover's with us. Rae would have loved the hell out of—" His smile died along with his words as he turned and caught sight of Nila's face. "I guess I should have asked," he said hesitantly, "if it was okay to invite her over."

Nila drew in a deep breath before saying carefully, "This is your home too. You do not need permission to invite your friends to visit." She smiled, but it was forced. A terrible sense of foreboding had entered her bloodstream and was making straight for her brain.

"Are you sure?" he asked, looking at her with concern. "I think you'll like Rae."

"I'm sure it's all right, and I'm sure I'll like her just fine." But she wasn't certain of that last statement, because she had a terrible feeling Rae had been sent to talk Jake into returning to his old way of life. "Coffee," she said brightly. "I should put on a pot of coffee. Or do you think Rae would prefer wine?"

"She's a coffee addict." Jake ran his hand over his hair and frowned. "I get the feeling you feel threatened in some way by Rae. Why?"

"Well, maybe just a little." What an understatement that was! "I'm worried about the possibility she might have been sent here to talk you into reconsidering your retirement."

"Come here, Nila." Jake's voice deepened as he spoke her name, becoming rich and thick as honey. His gaze held hers as she walked toward him.

He clamped his hands gently around her wrists and drew her close. "Tell me you love me," he ordered softly.

The demand surprised Nila. "You know I do."

"Then say it."

She hesitated. "Don't you think it's ironic that a man who professes not to believe in love should enjoy hearing those three little words so much?"

"You believe in it." He brushed a coaxing kiss across her mouth. "And you're right, I do enjoy hearing those words from you. Tell me."

She sighed. "All right. I love you."

"If you love me, then why don't you believe I'm through working for the DEA?" He cocked an eyebrow inquiringly.

The doorbell saved Nila from answering that loaded question. "Rae's here. Go let her in, Jake?"

Wordlessly, he released her.

Nila watched him leave the room, wondering what they would be letting into their lives when he opened the front door.

• • •

Nila sat near Jake on the sofa, a cup of coffee in her hand and her heart in her throat. Nothing Jake had ever said about Rae Garcia had prepared her for the lovely Spanish rose sitting across from them in a wing chair.

At first Nila had had a difficult time imagining this small, delicate, fine-featured woman in the role of undercover agent. Sitting there in her expensive tailored slacks and jacket, with straight midnight-black hair flowing past her shoulders, Rae could have been a fashion model or actress. Her eyes were the color of warm brandy, and her manner was open and friendly.

Eventually, though, Nila realized the woman possessed the same alert and watchful quality that was so much a part of Jake. She had a feeling she had been assessed, analyzed, catalogued, and categorized within minutes of meeting Rae.

And yet Nila found it impossible not to like her. Rae's affection for Jake was genuine, and she seemed to approve of his plans for the future as well as his relationship with Nila.

Rae set her coffee cup on the butler's table beside her and got down to the real purpose of her sudden visit. "I need your help, Jake. You know I wouldn't ask if there was any alternative." In order to penetrate one of the toughest crime organizations in Miami, she went on, she needed Jake's help to win the confidence of an informant who would deal only with "the Mad Man."

No! Nila thought wildly, when Jake didn't immediately refuse his help. "What if something goes wrong?" she asked, unable to keep silent any longer. In her mind she saw another psycho aiming a gun at Jake. What if it should happen again? What were his chances of escaping death a second time?

He gave her a reassuring smile. "Nothing will go wrong, sweetheart. My part of the job is a piece of cake. All I have to do is talk to the informant."

"What I'm asking Jake to do isn't dangerous," Rae said, also offering Nila a smile filled with reassurance and understanding sympathy.

Nila had a terrible feeling that their notion of danger was vastly different from her own.

As Jake and his former partner began to discuss possible ways to handle the situation after getting Rae accepted by the organization, a dreadful pressure built up in Nila's chest, a pressure so painful she bit into her lower lip to keep from crying out. Jake was talking as though he were back in the undercover business. Surely he wouldn't go back and put himself on the line again. He'd told her he wouldn't!

Dread filled her. Looking at Jake and Rae, she realized how much alike they were. The light of battle shone in their dark, calculating eyes. Their body language spoke of intense mental alertness and the thrill of the impending hunt.

She knew then that death wasn't the only way she could lose Jake. The job was in his blood. It would be so easy for him to get sucked back into that seductively dangerous world.

Nila had the strangest desire to escape up to the attic and lock the door, as she had the day her daddy packed his bags and left. But she wasn't a devastated child any longer. She was a woman who knew how to hide her feelings, a woman who knew how to be polite and gracious even in the worst of situations.

So she played the good hostess, went out to the kitchen and made sandwiches to serve with more coffee. And she died a little inside.

An hour later, Nila threw herself into Jake's arms as soon as the door closed behind their guest. "Don't do it. Please don't do it."

Jake held her close. He had been dreading this moment. Although she had maintained a pleasant facade throughout Rae's visit, he had tuned in on her mounting tension, and he had caught flashes of terror in her eyes.

"It's all right, sweetheart," he murmured, his mouth against her hair as she clung to him. "Tell me what you're afraid will happen."

Her voice shaking, she told him her concerns, and he listened with growing dismay. When she finally wound down, he guided her back to the sitting room and pulled her down with him on the blue-and-white striped sofa. He cradled her in his arms. "What I'm going to do won't put me in danger. All I have to do is talk the little weasel into working with Rae. From there, I'm out of the picture. The difficult part of the scam will fall on Rae's shoulders."

He didn't tell her how worried he was about the danger his friend would face alone. This was a job he himself would have been reluctant to take on even in his earliest, craziest days with the DEA.

"Why can't Rae talk the informant into helping her?" Nila asked. "Why does she need you?"

"Because he doesn't know her. He doesn't trust her yet. He knows me. I have to go back and do this one last thing."

She pulled back to face him, her eyes blazing with anger. "You don't *have* to do anything. You *want* to do it, don't you?"

"Yes. I want to."

"Dammit, Jake." She covered her face with her hand.

He held her tightly as she trembled with an effort not to cry. "I left a big unresolved issue when I walked away from the job," he said, struggling for a way to express his feelings. "I thought I would control the darkness, but it controlled me through the nightmare because I never really faced up to my own fears. I let my fear of crossing over the edge spook me into running. Don't you see, sweetheart? This is an opportunity for me to go back and face that fear. It's a chance to prove to myself that I am a decent human being, a chance to prove that I can function even in this small way on the job without letting that fear rule me. Only then can I make an honest choice to walk away from it. It's like getting back on the horse that's thrown you."

An emotional barrage stoked the fire of Nila's anger. "What a crock! Falling off a horse and walking away from a gun that miraculously jammed cannot possibly compare."

"Dammit, Nila, don't make this any harder than it already is. What I'm trying to explain is that if I don't get back in the saddle, I risk being controlled by that fear for the rest of my life. *I* need to know that I control the fear. Afterward I can choose to never do it again."

Her shoulders slumped with resignation. There was nothing she could say or do to prevent him from going back to Miami with Rae.

Nila squeezed her eyes shut. If only he loved her, she might be able to believe he could resist the lure of undercover work. But he didn't love her. All he truly needed from her was a good night's sleep.

If he didn't need her to keep the nightmare away, why should he come back to her?

"Come on, sweetheart. It's late. Let's go to bed."

It was the wrong thing to say. Hurt, confusion, and sexual tension mixed with her anger, producing an uncontrollable emotional turmoil. Her eyes flew open. "Why? So you can have one last peaceful, demon-free night's sleep? Well, maybe I don't want you in my bed tonight."

He didn't exactly push her out of his way, but he got to his feet so suddenly it seemed as though he did. "Fight with me if you want, but fight fair."

"Fair?" she shouted, jumping up. "You haven't fought fair since I met you!" It wasn't true. She knew that in her heart, but she was too upset to care.

His mouth hardened into a grim line. "Is it too much to ask for a little trust and faith?"

The bleak expression on her face answered his question.

"I guess it is." His eyes went cold as he steadily held her gaze. "You don't trust your own judgment, so why should you trust mine? You don't have much faith in yourself. Why should you have any in me?"

He spun around and stalked out of the room, leaving Nila feeling sick at heart.

Later she lay awake, staring at her bedroom ceiling. When she had insisted on sleeping alone, she hadn't thought about the darkness or how empty the bed would feel without him.

And now . . .

The night was darker than she'd ever known.

The bed felt as big and empty as the tremendous black sky outside her window.

And the loneliness . . .

Nila had dealt with losses before, but none of them were quite as horrible as the possibility that Jake would walk out of her life and never come back.

The next morning he came to say good-bye.

Nila was stiff and distant with him. She didn't want to be, but she couldn't help it.

"I know you're scared," he said, his voice betraying his own tense emotions. "Whether you believe it or not, I am coming back."

She willed herself not cry, but a tear sneaked past her guard, and she lowered her head to hide it.

It didn't work. She felt his thumb brush against her damp cheek.

He gently pulled her into his arms. "Remember, I'm the man who wanted you the first time I saw you. I'm the same man who wanted to own you after the first time we made love. I tracked you down when you ran away and I followed you home. In some crazy way, I think I've been searching for you all my life. You're a gift I refuse to part with."

In spite of her determination to remain aloof, his words, tugged at her heart. She realized, almost miraculously, that he did love her even if he didn't think he did.

He rubbed his thumb across her lips, then stepped back. His searching gaze roved over her face for a long moment. "So far, I've made all the moves. It's your turn, Nila. I need to know you trust me enough to believe my feelings for you are real and lasting. When my business in Miami is finished, I'll send you a plane ticket. If you want me, you'll have to come to me in Freeport-Lucaya. I'll wait for you in the casino."

The day dragged by after Jake left. Nila blindly walked through the routine of opening the shop, wanting to cry every time she thought of how badly she had behaved. She hadn't even kissed him good-bye.

All too soon Emma, Clover, and Angie descended upon her, ready for a hot cup of coffee and eager to discuss the previous day's Thanksgiving gathering.

Nila took one look at them and burst into tears. She gladly went into the comforting arms of her mother.

Emma held her, smoothing her hair while she poured out a watery, halting version of what had happened.

"Didn't I tell you men are the scourge of the earth," Clover said. "Cheer up, Nila Ann, things could be worse."

"Oh, shut up," Angie snapped. "I swear, you have the sensitivity of a fence post. Jake isn't running out on her."

"Of course he isn't." Emma patted her daughter's back. "Pull yourself together, baby. I know you don't want to hear this, but Jake is right. You're allowing your fears to control you."

"You're supposed to be on my side, Mama." Nila accepted the box of tissues Angie handed her. She ripped one out and blew her nose loudly.

"I am on your side. You just don't want to face the facts." Emma's lower lip trembled slightly. "In a way, I'm to blame for that."

Nila frowned. "What are you talking about?"

She sank down into the chair beside the coffee display.

"Jake knows the wisdom of facing his fears. That's something I never learned to do, something I never taught you or your sister. When your father left me, I felt as though I wasn't pretty enough, smart enough, special enough to hold on to my husband. What I didn't want to accept was that those superficial qualities had nothing to do with the reason he left. So I covered up my feelings of inadequacy by going to extremes to prove I was a desirable woman who could have her pick of any man she wanted. You hide your fear of abandonment and self-doubts in the same way, but on the opposite side of the spectrum."

Nila opened her mouth to defend herself, but closed it quickly. Everything her mother said was true.

She reached out her hand to Emma. "Thank you, Mama. You know I love you, don't you?"

Emma smiled as she gave her daughter's hand a squeeze. "Of course I do, baby. And I love you. Now, I want you to take two aspirins and go lie down until you've thought this thing through. Jake's a hell of man. It would be a real shame to let him get away. Angie can mind the store for a while."

She walked over to Clover and linked her arm through hers. "Let's go talk some trash. I heard from a very reliable source that you and Harmon Cook have been seen making goo-goo eyes at each other."

"Emma Margaret! I wouldn't give Harmon Cook the time of day if he got down on his scrawny little knees and begged me."

• • •

A week later, Nila walked into the Bahamas Queen Casino in Freeport-Lucaya. Once again she wore Angie's black velvet and emerald satin dress. Only this time she wasn't looking for a night of fantasy, she was searching for a reality. Her heart pounded as she stood at the edge of the gambling floor.

"Looking for a little bad company, lady?" a rich, intimately low voice said from behind her.

She slowly turned to face Jake. He looked so wonderful in the suit he'd worn before that her breath caught in her throat. A smile trembled on her lips.

"For the slot machine," he said, holding out a coin. "Play it one more time for me."

"I haven't been very lucky tonight," she answered as she had the first time she met him.

He smiled wickedly and dropped the quarter into her waiting palm. "I have a feeling your luck is about to change."

"You're all the luck I need." She took his hand, led him to the casino entrance, and out the door.

"I love you, Nila," he said as they headed toward the hotel complex.

She cast him an amused glance. "You didn't love me a week ago. What makes you think you love me now?"

He brought her to a halt, and she looked up at him.

Clouds floated from the face of the moon, whose beams penetrated through the palm trees and cast them in a radiant silver light. A soft island breeze whispered through the night.

"You made a believer out of a cynic." He touched her hair, caressed her cheek. "I've loved you since I woke up in my hotel room to find you gone. I was just too stubborn and set in my ways to recognize it."

"I love you too." She tilted her face up, inviting a kiss.

He didn't disappoint her. His lips moved druggingly over hers. "All I thought about this week was you," he murmured against her mouth. He raised his head and gazed into her eyes. "You give my life balance, passion, and love. In coming here to me, you've given me complete trust and loyalty. I want to give all those vital things and more back to you."

"Were you able to convince the informant to cooperate?" she asked, then smiled, knowing that was not what he'd expected her to say.

"Yes."

"Is the nightmare over?"

"For good."

"Then you don't need me to help you sleep."

"No, but my need for you is stronger, more urgent than ever."

"Are you going to marry me?"

"You bet." He lowered his head to kiss her again.

She wound her arms around his neck. "How do you feel about babies?"

The look he gave her was priceless. It was the stunned, fearful, and yet hopeful look men had been giving the women they loved since time began. "You're not . . . ?"

She laughed again. "No, but I'd certainly like to be. We have a lot of empty bedrooms waiting to be filled at home."

His arms went around her, warm, tender, inviting. His lips were hot on hers, very hot. The stroke of his tongue was slow and sensual.

No words passed between them, for the beauty of the moment was too wonderful.

Jake lifted his head at last. "Let's go, sweetheart. We've got babies to make."

And later that night, Jake smiled in the darkness as he held his sleeping love close. He had never imagined it could feel so good to love so deeply.

THE EDITOR'S CORNER

Soon we'll be rushing into the holiday season, and we have some special LOVESWEPT books to bring you good cheer. Nothing can put you in a merrier mood than the six fabulous romances coming your way next month.

The first book in our lineup is **PRIVATE LESSONS** by Barbara Boswell, LOVESWEPT #582. Biology teacher Gray McCall remembers the high school student who'd had a crush on him, but now Elissa Emory is all grown up and quite a knockout. Since losing his family years ago, he hadn't teased or flirted with a woman, but he can't resist when Elissa challenges him to a sizzling duel of heated embraces and fiery kisses. Extracurricular activity has never been as tempting as it is in Barbara's vibrantly written romance.

With **THE EDGE OF PARADISE,** LOVESWEPT #583, Peggy Webb will tug at your heartstrings—and her hero will capture your heart. David Kelly is a loner, a man on the run who's come looking for sanctuary in a quiet Southern town. Still, he can't hide his curiosity—or yearning—for the lovely woman who lives next door. When he feels the ecstasy of being in Rosalie Brown's arms, he begins to wonder if he has left trouble behind and finally found paradise. A superb love story from Peggy!

Only Jan Hudson can come up with a heroine whose ability to accurately predict the weather stems from her once having been struck by lightning! And you can read all about it in **SUNNY SAYS,** LOVESWEPT #584. Kale Hoaglin is skeptical of Sunny Larkin's talent, and that's a problem since he's the new owner of the small TV station where Sunny works as the weather reporter. But her unerring predictions—and thrilling kisses—soon make a believer of him. Jan continues to delight with her special blend of love and laughter.

Please give a rousing welcome to new author Deborah Harmse and her first novel, **A MAN TO BELIEVE IN,** LOVESWEPT #585. This terrific story begins when Cori McLaughlin attends a costume party and catches the eye of a wickedly good-looking pirate. Jake Tanner can mesmerize any woman, and Cori's determined not to fall under his spell. But to be the man in her life, Jake is ready to woo her with patience, persistence, and passion. Enjoy one of our New Faces of 1992!

Michael Knight feels as if he's been **STRUCK BY LIGHTNING** when he first sees Cassidy Harrold, in LOVESWEPT #586 by Patt Bucheister. A mysterious plot of his matchmaking father brought him to England, and with one glimpse of Cassidy, he knows he'll be staying around for a while. Cassidy has always had a secret yen for handsome cowboys, and tangling with the ex–rodeo star is wildly exciting, but can she be reckless enough to leave London behind for his Montana home? Don't miss this enthralling story from Patt!

Tonya Wood returns to LOVESWEPT with **SNEAK,** #587, and this wonderful romance has definitely been worth waiting for. When Nicki Sharman attacks the intruder in her apartment, she thinks he's an infamous cat burglar. But he turns out to be Val Santisi, the rowdy bad boy she's adored since childhood. He's working undercover to chase a jewel thief, and together they solve the mystery of who's robbing the rich—and steal each other's heart in the process. Welcome back, Tonya!

FANFARE presents four spectacular novels that are on sale this month. Ciji Ware, the acclaimed author of *Romantic Times* award-winner **ISLAND OF THE SWANS,** delivers

WICKED COMPANY, an engrossing love story set in London during the eighteenth century. As Sophie Mc-Gann moves through the fascinating—and bawdy—world of Drury Lane, she remains loyal to her dream . . . and the only man she has ever loved.

Trouble runs deep in **STILL WATERS,** a novel of gripping suspense and sensual romance by Tami Hoag, highly praised author of **LUCKY'S LADY.** When the body of a murder victim literally falls at Elizabeth Stuart's feet, she's branded a suspect. But Sheriff Dane Jantzen soon becomes convinced of her innocence, and together they must find the killer before another deadly strike can cost them their chance for love, even her very life.

In the grand tradition of **THORN BIRDS** comes **THE DREAMTIME LEGACY** by Norma Martyn, an epic novel of Australia and one unforgettable woman. Jenny Garnett is indomitable as she travels through life, from a childhood in a penal colony to her marriage to a mysterious aristocrat, from the harshness of aching poverty to the splendor of unthinkable riches.

Treat yourself to **MORE THAN FRIENDS,** the classic romance by bestselling author BJ James. In this charming novel, corporate magnate John Michael Bradford meets his match when he's rescued from a freak accident by diminutive beauty Jamie Brent. Mike always gets what he wants, and what he wants is Jamie. But growing up with six brothers has taught independent Jamie never to surrender to a man who insists on always being in control.

Also on sale this month in the hardcover edition from Doubleday is **LAST SUMMER** by Theresa Weir. The author of **FOREVER** has penned yet another passionate and emotionally moving tale, one that brings together a bad-boy actor and the beautiful widow who tames his heart.

The Delaneys are coming next month from FANFARE! This legendary family's saga continues with **THE DELANEY CHRISTMAS CAROL,** three original and sparkling novellas by none other than Iris Johansen, Kay Hooper, and Fayrene Preston. Read about three generations of Delaneys in love and the changing faces of Christmas past, present, and future—only from FANFARE.

Happy reading!

With best wishes,

Nita Taublib

Nita Taublib
Associate Publisher
LOVESWEPT and FANFARE

OFFICIAL RULES TO WINNERS CLASSIC SWEEPSTAKES